LYCAN MOON

Hearts on Fire
Book Two

Alexis Kennedy

ISBN: 978-1-946212-35-1
Title Wave Publishing LLC
Union, MO

http://bit.do/AlexisKennedy

Cover design by Xcite! DesignZ

www.titlewavepublishing.com

Books by Alexis Kennedy

Bound Through Blood

Under the Blood Moon (Hearts on Fire Book 1)

Ravaged (Dial M for Murder Book 1)

Déjà Vu (Dial M for Murder Book 2)

Cupid (Dial M for Murder Book 3)

Two Faced

Scandalous

Angry House

Birthright

Indelible (Two Faced book 2)

Gods and Angels

Lycan Moon (Hearts on Fire Book 2)

Dedicated to Crystal Galvan - smith

April 14, 2014
San Francisco, CA

Julia and Seth's wedding was just moments away, and she was trembling from her nerves. Madame Elmira and the other matriarchs of the clan were making a fuss over her, getting her ready for her groom.

They dressed her in an intricately designed Gypsy wedding dress that belonged to Madame Elmira. The woman had been saving it for her only niece, Ofelia.

"Are you sure you don't mind me wearing the dress?" Julia asked Ofelia. "I mean, it's meant for you."

Ofelia fingered the lace mermaid gown that hugged Julia's trim body perfectly. "Oh yes! It will be an honor to have a queen wear my dress," the young Gypsy responded with enthusiasm.

The bride bit her bottom lip. "Queen? That's going to take a lot of getting used to." She smiled nervously at the women who were putting a tiara and flowers in her hair.

Madame Elmira patted her arm reassuringly. "You're going to make a wonderful Lycan queen. Your destiny is of upmost importance, and it's just beginning."

Julia wished she felt as confident as the Gypsy. A lot was going to be expected of her in her new role as queen of the Lycans—such as helping to save the world. *But no pressure.*

"Your king is ready and waiting at the altar," Ofelia announced, causing Julia's stomach to flip.

She took a deep breath and started down the aisle, which was sprinkled with rose petals in an array of colors. Seth was positively gorgeous in the ornate robes he wore. His broad smile crinkled the area around his eyes, making him even handsomer than usual. Her legs wobbled as she approached him. She didn't know anything about being a wife, a queen, or a savior of mankind. *And what about children? What are Lycan babies like?* Her head began to spin, and Seth must have picked up on her unease because he winked at her encouragingly. The simple gesture, along with the intensity of his gaze, made her think all would somehow be okay. At least she'd have him by her side.

In what felt like a blink of the eye, the ceremony was over, and she was a Lycan queen. Gypsy performers entertained everyone during the reception. There was music and dancing, juggling acts, and even a sword swallower. The massive amount of food and drink was impressive too.

Then came the wedding night, and Julia felt like a virgin again. It was her first time making love as someone's wife, and that meant something special. It had deep meaning beyond gratification. She put on a sheer white nightgown for his enjoyment.

He pulled her close and whispered into her ear, "I love you so much, my queen, and I have since we first met. This is a dream come true for me."

She looked at him with soft eyes but a mischievous grin. "Even though blood-sucking vampires are a part of the package?"

He shook his head and returned her smile. "I'd fight every vampire out there if it meant being with you. Now, that's enough talk."

He slipped her nightgown off her shoulders and took a taut bud in his mouth. His hungry mouth then trailed a path down her trim body until he'd tasted all of her. She raked her fingernails across his massive shoulders while he brought her to quaking pleasure. Then he slid himself inside her molten center, and her gasps mingled with his growls while he prodded her pleasure point repeatedly.

Julia dug her fingernails into his rock-hard buttocks, urging him to thrust harder. He readily obliged, giving her everything she needed and more. Her screams filled the air while he drilled into her, rocking her in a sweet rhythm of release. Then his shout mingled with hers as his culmination crashed over hers like a tidal wave.

Panting, she nestled against his chest with his arm protectively wrapped around her. For once, she felt like she didn't have a care in the world. Vampires and impending battles were far from her mind as they drifted off to sleep.

April 15, 2014

Oscar's whimpers woke Julia and Seth up on their first morning as husband and wife. With a stretch and a yawn, she threw a questioning glance at her new husband.

He, in turn, looked at the pooch. "Okay, buddy, I guess Daddy will take you out."

"I'll make breakfast for you, my king, while you do that," Julia told him lovingly. "How does eggs and bacon sound?"

A large buck sounded better to the beast inside him, but he didn't want to hurt her feelings or scare her, so he playfully growled, "That sounds delicious, my darling queen. We'll be back in a few minutes."

He climbed out of bed and dressed to take Oscar out. While walking around the building, he sniffed the air, and so did the dog. It was clear of vampire stench, but he knew it wouldn't be for long. They were building their army, and he had to follow suit. The blood moon was coming that night, and he didn't have a single Lycan soldier in his army yet.

Before the wedding ceremony, the Gypsy clans had meshed to make plans. One of their plans was to help Seth locate other Lycans still in existence. The council had agreed to check the cards, crystal balls, and everything else at their disposal to locate the Lycans before it was too late.

With a sigh, Seth looked down at his quiet pendant. "You have to know where they are. Why aren't you talking to me?" he spoke to the necklace. "Don't let me down now." To his surprise, it grew warm. "Show me," he commanded it and closed his eyes.

He was shown a thick forest that housed a crude cottage. A large, naked man with blond hair emerged from the cottage and shifted before bolting through the trees.

Seth's eyes flew open. There was at least one, but he had to learn where the forest was. *Maybe Madame Elmira can help me find that cottage.*

He took Oscar back inside and discussed the vision with Julia over breakfast.

"Well, I guess it wouldn't hurt to ask her. Or do you think Ofelia would have the answer? She's the key after all," she suggested.

Seth put down his fork and stared at her with admiration sparkling in his brown eyes. "You're very smart, my bride. I think asking Ofelia is a wonderful idea. If she can't figure it out, she should know who can."

After Julia cleaned up the breakfast mess, they got ready to go into town. "We need to get your things from James's house, so you can move in here all the way," she mentioned. "The sooner the better. I'm sure his family is trying to sell the place."

He looked at her and saw tears pooled in her beautiful blue eyes. "Again, I'm so sorry about killing your friend. I had to protect my secret, and he'd seen me."

She shook her head and replied, "I don't want to talk about it. I just want to forget it, okay? Let's go there before we go to the Gypsy camp."

"Of course, my darling. I just want to make you happy," he sighed. "Luckily, I don't have much there. I only have a few outfits."

Her lip turned up in the corner. "Well, then I guess I need to take you shopping."

He chuckled, "That sounds like fun." He reached over and took her right hand in his left and stroked the top of it. He noticed her trembling. "What's wrong, darling? I can feel you quivering."

She glanced at him when she reached a red light. "Tonight is the blood moon. We haven't even had time to honeymoon before all hell breaks loose. Furthermore, I tried to call Melanie while you walked Oscar, and her phone is turned off. I'm really worried about her. I need to tell her what Brad has done, but I'm not sure how."

Seth nodded. "I understand, and I agree that she needs protection. I need to take care of Brad before he hurts more Gypsies too. You do understand that, right?"

She was driving again but shot him a quick glance. "I thought we'd turn him into the police," she squawked. "Let them make sure justice is served."

Seth ran his hand across his jaw. "I'm afraid it's not that easy, sweetheart. There's no proof we can show the police to make sure he's arrested. They can't know about vampires and Lycans—the world isn't ready for it. Also, since he's working with vampires, that makes him especially dangerous. My hands are tied, and he'll be a casualty of battle. I have to protect you," he explained.

Julia sighed and swallowed the lump in her throat. "Okay, whatever you think is best. I trust you." She bit her bottom lip while a question formed. "What are you going to do with the Lycans when you find them? I mean, where will they all stay? We certainly don't have the room in my apartment."

"Hmm…I suppose they might be able to stay at the Gypsy camp," he suggested. "We can ask about that while we're there."

She pulled into James Harvey's driveway and waited in the car while Seth retrieved his belongings. She didn't bother to ask him how he'd paid for the clothes; she had a hunch he'd used James's money. It was lucky for Seth that James's closest relatives lived in Canada, or they might have discovered his presence. She was surprised he'd kept it from the local police.

She looked at the Lycan king as he walked back to the car. She was heartbroken over James's early and horrific demise, but she loved her new husband, so she had to push her unpleasant thoughts aside. She couldn't let it hang over their marriage like a dark cloud, and she believed that he felt guilty. He was trying to save mankind after all.

"This is everything I have," he announced while throwing his belongings into the back seat.

She shook her head at him. "Tsk-tsk. That will never do for a king," she teased.

He laughed, "Married one day, and she already wants to change me."

Julia laughed with him, but she was mentally picking out clothing stores to visit. It would have to be a big and tall store no matter what, and she knew of a couple in the city.

When they arrived at the Gypsy camp in Chinatown, they quickly sought out Ofelia.

"Can we sit down and talk for a bit?" Seth asked the young woman.

Ofelia nodded. "Oh, sure. Come into my tent, unless you need the council members present too."

His brows furrowed. "We might be able to do this without them. Let's find out." He and Julia followed her inside her immaculate quarters. "I had a vision this morning of another Lycan, but I can't determine where he's located. I'm hoping you can help with that," he explained. "Then perhaps he'll know of others."

Ofelia pointed for them to sit in the metal chairs she had set out, while she sat on the ground in front of them. "How did you have your vision?"

He looked down at the pendant of λύκος and replied, "My magical pendant showed me when I asked it to. However, it didn't show me enough to determine the Lycan's location. That's where I hope you can help. It was Julia's idea, actually, since you are the key."

She sighed, "It's a lot of pressure to be told I'm the strongest Gypsy in all of history, but I'll accept my destiny with pride, and I'll do the best I can, so I don't let everyone down."

"I understand your concerns," Julia sympathized. "I feel the pressure too."

Seth looked at his bride and then at Ofelia. "You are two special women, and everything will work out fine. You wouldn't have been entrusted with your roles if you couldn't handle them."

"I just hope you're right," Ofelia whispered in a husky voice. "Now, let's see if I can get your vision, so I can help you. If not, I'll check around with the council to see what they can do."

He nodded and closed his eyes while grasping his pendant. He spoke to it in Romanian. "Descuie viziunea vârcolacului pe care mi l-ai arătat înainte. Deblocați-l și partajați-l cu noi din nou."

Unlock the vision of the Lycan you showed me before. Unlock it and share it with us again.

Once the vision began for him, he handed the necklace to Ofelia. She held it and let the vision take her away. Her eyes were closed, and her eyebrows pulled tightly together as she studied the mental pictures. Then she reached out and placed one hand on her crystal ball.

"I'm getting a picture in my crystal ball, and it's of a sign. The sign reads Klamath Falls," she announced.

Julia typed it into the search engine on her phone and informed them, "That's about six hours away in Oregon. Even if we leave right away, though, we won't be back in time for tonight's blood moon."

Seth groaned, "I'd say we could send a couple of Gypsy men to him to explain, but it's better if the information comes directly from me"—he looked down at Ofelia—"Is there a way for you or someone in the council to locate others who are closer? And is there a way to get a message to the one in Oregon?"

Ofelia tapped her fingers on her crystal ball while she pondered his questions. "I think we need the advice of the council. Follow me to the meeting caravan, and then I'll round them up." She got up, and they followed her to the largest caravan, which was painted in rich reds and yellows. "You can wait inside for us," she stated and watched them as they climbed inside.

Julia smiled while looking around the caravan. For a small space, it was alive with old-world charm. There was a long table with eight chairs around it, a small sofa, and lots of vibrant décor. Aromatic candles burned, putting off a sweet smell of lilacs mixed with vanilla. Outside, someone was playing the violin, so Julia peeked out the window. He appeared to be playing for a fussy baby who was squirming in his mother's arms.

Seth put his hand on the small of her back and looked out the window too. "How long do you think it will be before we're holding a baby?" he asked with a grin.

She smiled wickedly. "I'm sure that woman would let you hold hers," she teased.

He cocked his head at her. "Are you not anxious to start our family?" His tone was serious, so she wiped the smile off her face and stood up straighter.

"Well, this is all happening so fast. Can we wait a while before expanding our family? I'd like to have some alone time with my husband first. Besides, it doesn't mean we can't spend lots of time practicing," she told him.

He looked down and kept his tone light. "I think the prophecy demands we start right away, but we can double check with the Gypsies to be sure. I'd like alone time with you too, but I admit that I'm anxious to see our love born in a child."

Her heart melted when she saw the look on his handsome face. It was endearing. She instinctively reached up and touched him lovingly.

"I'd like to see that too," she whispered.

The door to the caravan swung open, and Madame Elmira announced, "Hello, young lovers. Third party entering the room." She climbed into the caravan and flashed them both a bright smile. "The other members of the council are right behind me."

"Good morning, Madame Elmira," Julia and Seth replied in unison.

She waved them off. "Please, just call me Elmira. I only use the Madame title at my shop to give me more credibility."

They nodded in understanding. "Did Ofelia fill you in?" Julia wondered.

The matronly Gypsy sat at the long table and nodded. "Yes, she explained that she shared your vision, and you want to know what we saw when we consulted the cards and such."

"That sums it up," Seth affirmed just as more council members climbed into the caravan.

Elmira and Ofelia explained what they were doing there, and they all sat down to discuss the possibilities.

ᛒrad paced his house nervously while Melanie sat on his sofa. "Will you stop pacing in circles?" she snapped.

He shot her an icy glare. "You are new to this, cousin, so you don't know what's on the line. That witch killed our bride for the vampire prince, so what do we do now? Do we just let her go and present herself to him?" he screeched. "I'm going to look incompetent."

Melanie rolled her eyes. "Yes, I suggest you let the bitch do just that. It's not your fault she killed the Gypsy girl. You held up your end of the deal when you found her for him."

Brad wanted to slap the woman. "It is exactly my fault that she was taken from my custody by the witch! I failed the prince, and he will surely not let me live with it."

"Didn't you say that vampire girl chased you from your house?" she asked.

His lip turned up. "You know, you might be more useful than I anticipated. Yes, she did, so it's her fault the witch took Ofelia. Hopefully, Prince Armando will at least see it that way."

Melanie rose from the couch and paced the room, looking over his occult books and paraphernalia. "So, what now? What do we need to do today to get ready?"

He stared hard at her while she fondled his potion bottles. "You need to learn more about the craft, so we'll spend the day studying. You need to be ready to assist the prince once I wake him."

She gave him a catty smile. "And how come *you* get to wake him?"

He shook his head with a sigh. "Because it's the prophecy that the oldest living Rosci clan member gets the privilege, and that's me."

She glanced down at the lush green carpet. "Speaking of our clan, since it's just us, who will carry it on?"

He grinned sadistically. "Oh, you never know. I may have knocked Julia's sweet ass up"—he clapped his hands together with a loud slap—"Of course, if she is pregnant, I'll have to abduct the child to make sure it is raised correctly, and if it turns out to be a mutt, I'll just dispose of it."

She grimaced at him. "Aren't you sweet?"

"I'll do what's necessary," he answered with a casual shrug. He eyed her head to toe. "However, there is another option."

"Why are you staring at me like that? You look like a predator," she remarked.

He reached out and squeezed her shoulder. "If we had a child, it would be a strong clan member with rich Rosci blood."

Melanie cringed. "Ew! You're my cousin!"

Brad rolled his eyes at her and let go of her shoulder. "We are third cousins, which makes it legal and not inbreeding."

She huffed, "Just the same, I'm in no rush to get knocked up by *anybody*."

He looked at her skeptically. "Even if it was by the Lycan king? I can tell you have a crush on the fleabag."

She shivered. "No, not anymore. Julia ruined that for me."

Brad fondled the Black Dragon amulet. "I suppose they're married by now too. Oh well. It just makes the competition more interesting."

She arched a brow. "The *competition?*"

"To rule the world."

ꝺMadame Elmira called the council meeting to order. "Yesterday, you were all asked to use the methods at your disposal to find other Lycans. Has anyone been successful?"

Grim expressions went around the table along with head shaking. Apparently, their efforts had been futile.

"I have an idea," Seth announced and stood up from the small sofa. "My pendant helped earlier, so if we combine its magic with yours, maybe we'll see what we need to." He glanced out at the sun, which was already starting its descent in the sky. "We should hurry too."

Elmira bustled about the caravan, pulling crystal balls, tarot cards, candles, and crystal pendants out of cabinets. She set them on the table in front of the other council members, and they spread everything out. The members clasped hands with each other and stared at Seth.

He chanted to the magical pendant, asking once again for its guidance. Smoke from the candles swirled around the caravan, and hazy images appeared to the Gypsies in the crystal balls.

"There is a small pack near Santa Maria. That's not too far from here," Ofelia announced.

"It's a four-hour drive," Julia offered and held up her phone.

Seth ran his hands through his hair. "I can't go today, though. I have to be here for when the vampire prince wakes. It's too late to stop the ceremony, but I have to be around to protect those whom I can."

"I'll go," Ofelia declared. "and I'll take volunteers from the council with me. They'll listen to us if we go in numbers, and I'll tell them about the pendant of λύκος. We'll explain about the vampire prince's ceremony, and then we'll bring them back with us. They can stay here in the camp as our guests." Her tone was confident, not leaving much room to argue with her. She was fitting into her role as the divined Gypsy leader.

"You're very brave," Seth commented with admiration.

She shrugged and replied, "I don't have a choice, do I?"

"None of us do, darling," Elmira sighed.

Four of the council members agreed to go with her, and they were quickly on their way. She took a cell phone with Seth and Julia's numbers stored in it, so she could call with their progress.

"You call if there is any trouble, too," Seth advised. "I can talk to the tribe over the phone if need be."

Elmira gathered other clan members to seek the lone Lycan in Klamath Falls. They also took a phone in case there was trouble with the beast.

"Be especially careful with that one," Seth advised. "There is a reason he's not with a pack, unless I just didn't see the others in my vision."

"Now what?" Julia asked him as they made their way back to her apartment. "What do we do tonight?"

She saw his grimace out of the corner of her eye. "We can only wait. We can pray and just wait."

April 15, 2014
Night of the Blood Moon

After a few spoken words, some spilled blood, and a thousand years of lying in wait, dark eyes opened to the blackness of night. The vampire prince, Prince Armando, rose from his crypt and greeted his followers. Brad, Melanie, and Tressa were among them.

Zephryne approached him first. "Good evening, my future king. I have prepared a small army for your arrival, and we have your bride here as well to complete the prophecy." She turned to Tressa and said, "Come forth witch."

"Witch?" he growled, "I do not recall there being a witch in the prophecy I was foretold before my rest."

"I am a dark Gypsy, who turned to witchcraft to harness my power," Tressa stated and stepped forth. "My power combined with yours, of course, will tear down the Lycan army and sweep across the world in a plague." She gave him a vindictive smile.

"So, the Lycans have fulfilled their end of the prophecy as well? The king is awake and has found his queen?"

Tressa was the one who answered because Brad was too nervous to speak. "Yes, the king is awake, but I'm sure he will be no match for you—for us. I do not know if he has found his queen or not. The only good Gypsy strong enough to be queen is now fish food. The dark Gypsy"—she pointed to Brad—"was going to bring her here for you, but I knew she would never suffice. I am the only one strong enough to carry out your wishes, my lord." She bowed before him. "Now, shall we say our dark vows and anoint you King Armando?"

He smiled at the pretty witch. "Yes, but I'm famished." He grabbed Tressa's arm and pulled her into his iron embrace while he sank his fangs into the soft skin on her neck. He drained her completely while the others watched and then let her lifeless body sink to the ground. "Get rid of the cocky bitch," he told Zephryne. Then he turned to Brad and said, "I don't doubt that you have found a suitable queen for me."

"But the witch killed her, my lord," Brad uttered and nervously shuffled his feet.

"No, she's right here." The dark prince looked squarely at Melanie.

"What?" Melanie and Brad both squawked.

Armando reached out a boney hand adorned with long fingernails and stroked her cheek, causing her to cringe in fear. He smiled, showing off his razor-sharp fangs.

"You are perfect to be my queen. I can read it on your black heart," he hissed with a lusty grin. "Unfortunately, this is going to sting, but then you'll soon feel much better."

He snatched her wrist before she could pull it away and sank his fangs into her tender flesh. He took several long pulls on her crimson nectar before letting her go with a malicious chuckle.

Melanie fell to her knees from the weakness that suddenly overcame her. Her head spun, and her heart beat sluggishly in her ears. She felt death coming. Something went by in a blur out of the corner of her eye, and it took everything left in her to look up to see what it was. The vampire girl, Zephryne, had a wriggling human in her iron embrace.

"Perfect timing, my dear," Prince Armando cooed to the vampire.

He grasped the scrawny man from her clasp and tore into his neck. Then he threw the convulsing body at Melanie.

"Feed your thirst, my queen. It will give you the strength you crave," he commanded.

At first, the idea made her stomach lurch; however, once the metallic stench of blood filled her nostrils, she began to salivate. She lunged at the writhing man and gulped copious amounts of blood. Her face flushed, and her heart pounded with a new strength as the warm liquid ran down her throat. The prince was right—she craved it.

He pulled her off the dead man by her arm. "That's enough, love. Now, it's time for our vows"—he looked at Brad—"You'll, of course, conduct the ceremony."

Brad held up his book of black magic and flipped to the section he needed to perform the wedding. It was a short service, sealed with a kiss as all weddings were. Prince Armando licked the remaining traces of blood from Melanie's lips when he kissed her.

"Before we start the honeymoon, I'll be anointed King Armando," he declared, and Brad found the words necessary to perform the ritual. It, too, was over quickly.

"My king," Zephryne stated, and they all bowed to him and his queen.

Once they rose, Armando told Zephryne to take the others and recruit more soldiers for his army while he consummated his marriage to Melanie.

Melanie trembled in fear as he led her off to the cover of trees in the nearby cemetery. It was one hook-up she could do without.

April 16, 2014

Julia climbed out of bed without waking Seth up. She took Oscar out for his morning walk and then started cooking breakfast. While the sausage sizzled, she dialed Melanie again. Her friend hadn't bothered to return her calls, and her concern was growing. It went straight to voicemail again.

"Melanie, it's Julia. I'm really worried about you, so please call me back as soon as you get this. I need to talk to you about something urgent." She hung up just as she heard Seth stirring in the bedroom.

"Good morning, my earth angel," Seth greeted her and gave her a kiss on the forehead. "Who are you calling? Did you hear from Ofelia or the others?"

He pulled his phone out of his pocket and checked for messages, but he didn't have any.

"No, I was calling Mel again. Her phone is still going to voicemail, though, and I'm worried. What can we do?" she asked.

He stuck his hands in his pockets. "I'm not sure. Did you leave a message for her?"

"I've left four messages for her now," Julia sighed. "What if Brad hurt her or worse?"

Seth wrapped his arms around her and gave her a comforting squeeze. "We can go by her house or where she works later if you want. We'll figure it out, or we can notify the police, okay?"

She looked up into his concerned face with tears in her blue eyes. "Okay. Thank you."

"Did you walk Oscar?" he wondered.

"Yes, I took him out a few minutes ago," she answered.

"How did he behave? Did he act strange?" He looked at the dog, who was napping on the living room floor.

Julia looked at her friend too. "No. He just did his business as usual."

"That's good. That means he didn't smell the stink of vampires," he acknowledged. "Still, I'm going to go out and check for myself. I won't go into the woods, though. I'll be right outside the building."

"Hurry back please," she called out after him. Oscar might be relaxed, but she was on pins and needles.

Her husband returned a few minutes later. "All clear for now," he sang out and locked the door behind him. "You know, to be on the safe side, it wouldn't hurt to install an alarm system."

She chuckled, "You mean you don't consider Ossy to be an effective alarm system?"

Seth bent over and rubbed the dog's ears. "I know that he'd give his last breath to save you, but I fear it's not enough. I want an alarm to alert you if necessary. I want you to know if Brad or a blood-sucker is trying to break in."

She scowled at the mental images. "Speaking of which, what would I do? If you weren't here to protect me, how would I save myself?" She pleaded with her eyes for a reassuring answer.

He sat at the table and rubbed his jaw. "Do you own a gun?" he inquired.

"No," she exclaimed. "Guns frighten me. I'm afraid I'll accidentally fire it."

He shrugged. "Well, you really should get one and learn how to shoot it. Let's go to the store today and then the firing range for practice. I need you to be able to protect yourself if I'm gone for some reason."

She cocked her head at him. "Would a gun even be effective against a vampire?"

"No, it's more complicated than that to kill a vampire, but it would be effective against the dark Gypsy."

She carried the plates of food to the table. "I suppose you're right about that, but I just don't know if I can kill another person," she replied in a trembling voice.

He reached out and patted her wringing hands. "You can if it means saving your life. Don't forget that he's a murderer. You'll do what you have to do."

She took a deep breath and sighed, "You're right. Now, what about vampires? How do you kill them?"

He looked down at his plate of steaming sausage and eggs. "The same way you kill a Lycan—decapitation."

Julia shivered with a sour expression. "Ew! That's awful, and I don't think I could do that."

In between bites of his food, he assured her, "You won't have to. It's up to the Lycans to stop the vampires. Also, the Gypsies can help because it's their battle too. All you need to do is keep yourself safe." He winked at her, hoping it would help calm her nerves. He hated making her a part of the colossal mess.

She bit her lip and then asked, "So, holy water, wooden stakes, sunlight, and crucifixes don't work to kill them like it does in the movies?"

He laughed and shook his head. "Well, not to my knowledge, but then we didn't have television back in my day."

She made a sour face, causing his laughter to grow. "I forgot how old you technically are. Speaking of which, how long do Lycans live? Are you immortal like vampires?"

He shrugged. "No one really knows because no Lycan—at least not in my time—died of natural causes. They only died in battle."

She studied his face. "Do you age, though? I mean, did your parents grow older as you grew up?"

He nodded. "Yes, we do age, but it is a slower process for us than humans."

Julia swung her head side to side. "So, I'm going to be older than you eventually, huh? I'm already twenty-eight."

He smiled. "Don't worry about that, my darling. When mortal women bear Lycan children, the aging process begins to slow for them as well. Besides, I'm still older than you—I was born in 1781."

"Wow," she whispered. "You're an old fart."

He laughed, causing his eyes to crinkle. "I suppose so. Now, how about we get ready to go to town? We'll get your gun and check on your friend."

"And get you some new clothes," she added with a grin.

He playfully slapped her on the bottom when she walked by him. "And what do old farts wear? Something like plaid?"

They purchased him some new clothes first. Then they stopped at a small gun and ammo store to shop for a handgun. They chose a 9mm for her, and she went behind the building to the small range for target practice. Surprisingly to her, she had good aim, so she didn't practice for long. Seth took a turn with the gun, even though he would use his inborn traits for self-preservation. With his exceptionally keen eyesight, he hit the bullseye each time.

"Show off," Julia teased.

He held his hands up in self-defense. "I can't help it if I have an advantage. Now, how about checking on Melanie? Do you want to call her first or just go by her house or work?"

She sighed and pulled her phone out of her purse. "Let me try calling." The phone went straight to voicemail again. "All right. I guess we'll go by her house and then the bank where she works. I'm going to slap her silly when we find her, though."

They climbed into her car and drove the four miles to Melanie's apartment building. She banged on the door, but no one answered. When the neighbor peeked outside her own door to scowl at her for the noise, she took advantage of it.

"I'm sorry, but I'm worried about Melanie. I'm her best friend, and I've not heard from her lately. Have you seen her coming or going?" she asked the elderly woman.

The woman shook her feeble white-haired head. "No. It's been nice and quiet for a change," she grumbled. "I've not heard a peep from her place in a couple of days. I'm rather enjoying it."

Julia searched Seth's face for his reaction. "Let's go to the bank then," he said and rubbed her arm to calm her nerves.

She took his hand in hers and squeezed it. "Speaking of work, I need to call in and let them know I won't be in today. It's great that I have a ton of vacation time saved up." She pulled her phone out and got her administrative assistant on the line.

"Marisol, I'm going to take at least another few days off, but it might be longer. I'll let you know. If the other partners ask, just tell them that I'm taking vacation time for personal reasons and send my clients to them. There should only be a couple who are filing extensions."

"Okay, I'll tell them. Mr. Vaughn hasn't been in either, and he left a message that he was taking time off too. I guess it's the stress of tax season," she surmised.

"I guess so," Julia agreed, but she knew otherwise. When they hung up, she told Seth about Brad's absence.

"He's busy with the vampire prince. According to the prophecy, he was to be woken on the night of the blood moon, married off, and anointed king," he explained.

She quirked her brow at him. "It's funny how his destiny correlates with yours. I mean, you both had to be woken up, and you both had to find a queen."

He nodded. "Yes, it's quite similar. Odd, huh?"

She pulled into the bank parking lot and drove around, looking for Melanie's blue Escort. "I don't see her car, but maybe she's at lunch, so I'm going to go inside and ask."

Seth followed her inside where she spoke to the branch manager. "I'm Melanie's friend, and I'm concerned about her well-being. Did she show up today?"

The manager's face drew taut. "I'm normally not allowed to discuss such things for the safety of our employees, but I'm worried about her too. She hasn't been in for two days, and quite frankly, I'm going to have to terminate her if she doesn't call in today and explain her absence. I have a bank to run, and I need all my staff present for their scheduled shifts."

"I understand, and if I hear from her, I'll pass that along," Julia assured her while tearing up inside. Something had happened to her friend, and she had no idea what.

7

Melanie's eyes fluttered open in the crack of sunlight that was streaming through the window in Brad's guestroom. She looked to her left and saw the vampire king sleeping soundly, and she shrunk back in fear. The previous evening returned to her and left a sour taste in her mouth as bile rose in her throat. He'd advanced on her like a cheetah in heat, and she had to endure his ravenous touch. Even worse, she had to pretend to enjoy it. He was attractive, but she couldn't relax enough to desire his company. He was just too frightening.

Her tongue traced her teeth, and she jumped when she felt her pointy fangs. *What have you done to me?* She had been turned into a monster, an immortal predator.

King Armando stirred, and his red glare settled on her, making her wish she was still asleep.

"I'm glad to see you're awake," he growled. "I'm ready again." He flipped back the covers to show her his hardened flesh.

Trying to distract him, she asked, "How are we awake during the day? What about the sun?"

His eyes became slits. "What about it?"

She tossed a glance toward the window. "It's always been said that vampires sleep during the day because the sun will kill them."

He reached out with a clawed hand and caressed her hair, making her shiver. "While we are predominantly creatures of the night, the sun won't kill us. It's easier to hide, though, in the veil of darkness. The night is so mysterious—as are we, my pet." He licked his cold, pale lips and then made his advance on her.

Melanie tolerated sex with him again, but once it was over, she sprang from the bed. "I'm going to take a shower."

Brad passed her in the hallway. "How was the honeymoon, cousin?" he mocked.

She waved him off with a flick of her hand. "I don't want to discuss it."

"I'm going to make something for breakfast? Do you want anything?"

She turned and looked at him with a burning in her throat. "I want blood. Can you find me some, or shall I take yours?" She smiled, showing off her new set of fangs.

He held his hands up in self-defense. "I believe Zephryne is working on that, but if not, I'll see what I can do," he offered.

"See that you do," she commanded. "I'm sure the king will be hungry too."

After she'd dried off and dressed, Melanie found the others convened in the living room. Zephryne was among them, and she had a burly man in her clutches.

"Good morning, my queen," she addressed Melanie and bowed her head subserviently. "I'm sure you are hungry." She licked her own fangs.

"Yes, I'm famished. Is he for me?" Melanie murmured and approached the wide-eyed man, who was struggling to break away.

Armando answered, "Yes, darling, he is for you; however, I don't want you to drain him completely. I think we shall add him to our army."

She glanced at her husband. "All right, Armando, I won't."

She grabbed the man with her newfound strength and sank her fangs into his thick neck. She tore his carotid and slurped the warm, salty blood that spurted forth like a crimson fountain while the stench of copper filled her nostrils.

"That's enough, love," Armando chastised and pulled her off him. "Brad, come here and lend us some of your essence."

"Me?" Brad shrieked. "Are you going to let him kill me?" Beads of sweat rolled down his forehead, and his eyes had lost their color.

The king of vampires laughed. "No, poppet. He just needs a taste of mortal blood to seal his conversion."

Brad knew he had to comply, or it would cost him his life, so he tentatively approached them. Shaking, he held out his wrist to the king, and Armando bit it and then held it to the dying man's mouth.

Brad winced from the burning pain of Armando's fangs and then again when he felt the suction of the mortal's lips. After the man had a couple of swallows, he yanked it away.

"Is that enough?" he asked in a high-pitched squeal.

They all observed the man when he began panting loudly. He opened his mouth just enough to reveal blood-tinged fangs. "Can I have more?" he requested in a husky voice. "I'm starving."

Armando laughed. "I'm famished as well, so we shall go hunting."

"I'm sorry that I didn't save you anything," Melanie expressed with shame. "It was hard to stop myself, though."

Her husband laughed lightly. "It's all right, my queen. I know how difficult it is to cut off one's thirst. Besides, I miss hunting for my prey. It has been far too long"—he shot a look at Brad—"You'll take care of my bride in my absence."

Brad nodded. "Yes, of course, my king. I'll look after her."

Armando instructed Melanie, "Spare the dark Gypsy his life, my black-hearted darling. He might prove useful to me yet." Then he motioned for the new vampire and Zephryne to follow him out the front door.

Melanie looked at Brad. "So, what shall we do while they're hunting?"

Brad looked down at the kitchen towel he'd wrapped around his wounded wrist. "After I bandage this, I can share more information about our family with you."

She smiled cattily and narrowed her eyes. "Or we can go see if we can get Julia alone. I'm still hungry."

Ofelia called Seth shortly after they'd left the bank and told him she and the council members had just returned to the camp with four Lycans.

"That's great! What about the lone Lycan in Oregon? Are they back yet?" he wondered.

"No, I'm afraid not. I haven't heard from them either, so I'm concerned for their well-being. Is there anything you can do?" she pleaded.

Seth clenched his free hand into a fist. "Maybe. Let me think about it. We'll be at the camp in a few minutes." He gestured to Julia to take the next exit, so she could head toward Chinatown.

"Okay, we'll be gathered outside the council's caravan. Bye," Ofelia stated and hung up.

Seth filled Julia in on the conversation. "I'm glad they were able to convince the Lycans to leave their territory and that they are getting along with the Gypsies," he mentioned.

She shot him a quick glance. "Why wouldn't they get along? You have no issues with the clan members, and they threw us a beautiful wedding ceremony."

He explained, "Gypsies and Lycans weren't always cooperative in my time. We didn't put our differences aside until the common enemy—vampires—threatened us both.

I was surprised when I woke and found out about their respect for me."

She chuckled, "It's good to be king," just as she pulled into the Gypsy camp.

The four Lycans stood out among the Gypsies gathered around the council's caravan. They were tall and brawny like Seth, but not as handsome. Seth had the pendant of λύκος showing, so they'd recognize him as the prophesied king. He hoped, though, that he wouldn't have to fight whatever king was leading the clans in the present day. He'd much rather form an additional clan under his rule and then have them all fight side by side, even if that meant changing willing humans into Lycan soldiers.

The four newcomers looked at Seth and then spoke quietly among themselves. Seth gave Julia a reassuring glance and then approached the small clan.

"Hello and thank you for joining us. I'm told you've been apprised of the situation. Is that correct?" Seth asked.

The four men bowed their heads to him. "You are the prophesied king, King Seth. We are here to help you in any way that we can. We are told the vampire prince has also risen and claimed his throne," the largest of the group answered.

"You've been told correctly," Seth acknowledged. "Are there only four of you in your pack, or did the others not want to come?"

One of the others answered, "I'm Brody, and this is Lobo, Rahl, and Aric. Packs aren't as common in this time as they were in your time. There isn't even a ruler; you were the last king. If you want to find others, you'll have to flush out the ones who live in solitary."

Lobo, who was the largest of the four, added, "Of course, we do recognize you as king."

Seth clasped the other Lycan's shoulder. "We are all an army, or at least we will be. This is our fight, not just mine. The Gypsies are going to help us too. Together, we'll build a strong, untouchable clan, and we'll wipe the vampires out."

Aric asked Seth, "Have you already located any others we can recruit?"

"There is one man in Oregon who came to me in a vision. Several Gypsies went in search of him, and I'm hoping they'll be returning with him soon."

A loud commotion made them look behind Seth. The large blond man he'd seen in his vision was stomping behind the troupe of Gypsies that had gone to fetch him. He wore a scowl.

"I'm Gerrant, and I want to know who has summoned me," he shouted.

Milo, who was one of the Gypsy men, told Seth, "We told him about you and the battle that is coming, but he doesn't want to believe us. I was surprised when he came back with us."

Gerrant glanced at Seth, and his face contorted. "So, it's true? You are the cursed king?" he inquired.

Seth nodded. "I am him, and it's also true that the vampire king is awake and building his army while we speak. So, the question remains, will you fight with us?"

"I hate blood-suckers!" the large blond spat. "Yes, I'll fight with you."

Seth shook each man's hand. "I'm glad we're already making headway, and you have been invited to stay here in the Gypsy camp. You know"—he shot a glance at Ofelia, who was standing nearby—"my queen and I are across the city, so perhaps we should relocate here as well. I think it's best if we all stay together until this is over."

Ofelia smiled at his suggestion. "I think that is an excellent idea. We will prepare a lovely caravan for you if you'd like to go fetch your things."

"Yes, we'll go get our belongings and our dog. We'll be back in a while then," he responded. Just as he was walking toward Julia, one of the Gypsy men stopped him.

"My name is Yoska, and I want to join the Lycan clan. Will you turn me?" he questioned.

Seth eyed the man up and down. He was scrawny, but he would bulk up if turned. "Are you sure you want to be a Lycan? The call of the beast is fierce," he forewarned.

Yoska blushed and looked down at his feet. "As you can see by looking at me, I'm kind of weak. I will serve you best if I am turned into the beast."

Seth nodded. "That's true, and I will consider it while we go collect our things. You think more about it also, and if you still desire the change, we'll discuss it when we return."

"Fair enough, King Seth," the man chimed with a broad smile, and then he flounced off.

They were on the way back to the camp with Oscar and enough belongings to last for a while, when Julia fired off some questions.

"How do you turn a human into a Lycan? Will they live as long? Is it painful for them? Have you done it before?"

He held one hand up. "Whoa! I'll answer your questions, darling, but how about giving them to me one at a time?" he chuckled. "First of all, I can turn a human by infecting them with a bite. Therefore, it does hurt. I have never needed to do it before. Our Lycan clan in my time was large enough, but there were soldiers who'd been turned by other members of the clan. Only a purebred Lycan can turn a mortal. As for life expectancy, I assume they will start to age at a slower rate just like a mortal who bears Lycan young."

"Hmm…" she replied. "That's a lot to think about. I mean, making the choice to turn yourself into a ferocious monster like that can't be easy."

Seth sighed and squeezed her hand. "You need to realize that in my time, we lived off the grid for the most part. Mortal man wasn't our enemy or our prey like you see in your movies. We were only fighting with the vampires and evil witches."

"I'm sorry if you think I'm calling you a monster," she whispered. "I know what you're about, and you're my hero."

He patted her leg as she pulled into the Gypsy camp. "I'm trying to be your hero. Don't ever doubt that I want to be."

When Melanie turned on her phone, she had several messages from Julia and a couple from her boss at the bank. She ignored the ones from the bank, but she listened to Julia's panicky messages with a self-satisfied grin. *Aw...The little bitch cares about my well-being. Isn't she in for a surprise?*

They parked on the street adjacent to Julia's and walked the short distance toward her building. Brad noticed Melanie's sneer get worse as they drew closer.

"What is the scowl about? I figured you'd be smiling," he quipped.

Her frown deepened. "I smell the Lycan, and it reeks. I can also smell her damn perfume, and it just pisses me off. She's with him, and I'm with..." She didn't feel the need to finish her thought, lest her discontentment get back to Armando.

Brad surprised her with his laughter. "You don't realize how good you've got it. You are an immortal, beautiful creature of the night, but she is married to a mutt and will be breeding with him to produce pups. She'll eventually die, but not you. So what if you aren't in love or even attracted to the vampire king? If Seth and his army succeed, Armando won't be in your way anymore."

She hissed at him, "You imprudent moron! If they succeed, I'll be dead too!"

He held up a finger to silence her rant. "Not if you find a place to hide when the time comes. The king doesn't expect you to fight. At least I don't think he does."

She sucked in her bottom lip, accidentally nicking it on her fangs. The taste of blood made her throat burn from hunger again.

"That's not a bad idea," she acknowledged, "and you should come with me when I hide. That way our clan can continue with you."

Brad nodded in agreement. "I'll do as you wish, my queen."

She tossed him a hungry glare. "Right now, what I wish for is that little bitch's blood, so let's go get her."

"How? I'm sure the Lycan is with her," he pointed out.

Melanie tapped her finger to her temple in thought. "Tell her there is an emergency with me, and she has to come with you to help me. She's already worried about my welfare, so that should work on her. Then, if the Lycan follows her outside, we'll take him down together."

Brad smiled maliciously and headed inside the building while Melanie hid around the corner to lie in wait. She was salivating at the thought of her next meal. Seven minutes ticked by before she heard someone running down the metal stairs. She peeked around the corner, prepared to lunge just in case it was Julia, but Brad burst through the doorway by himself. He wore an expression of angst.

"Where is she?" Melanie hissed.

Brad jumped at first because he hadn't seen her. Then his eyes darted all around except for on her face, and he held his breath. He knew how upset she was going to be, and he didn't want to face her rage.

"Where is my meal?" Melanie demanded again.

Brad forced himself to steady his voice as he told her, "They aren't there. I broke the door in just to be sure, and it looks like they packed in a hurry. Drawers are empty, and her dog is gone."

"Shit! Where did he take her?" she thundered.

Brad shuffled his feet. "I don't know, but I'm sure we'll find out."

She steepled her fingers and narrowed her eyes to mere slits. "We'd better, or it's your *neck*."

Elmira and Ofelia helped Julia get their things settled in a luxurious caravan while Seth met with the Lycan and Gypsy men to discuss protecting the camp.

"This is a beautiful dwelling," Julia exclaimed while looking around the caravan, "but I don't want us to put anyone out. We can just stay in a tent. That would be fine for us."

Elmira flicked her hand at her. "Nonsense. This is my abode, and I welcome you to it. Nothing less would do for the king and queen of the Lycans."

Julia felt herself blush. "You don't have to treat us like royalty. We aren't like that."

"But you are royalty, and you need to acknowledge that in your heart to tap into your full power, just as I have accepted who I am—the leader of the Gypsy clan," Ofelia chimed in. "Our roles are important in making sure we all survive what is to come. You have to be a strong leader for your tribe, just as I have to be for mine."

Elmira nodded emphatically. "She's right about that. I couldn't have said it any better."

Julia studied their faces while she felt hers still burning. "I suppose you're right," she finally relented. "It's just that everything happened so fast. I mean, I only met Seth about a week ago. I haven't even told my family yet because they'd have me committed to a mental hospital.

I've never been serious about a man before, and now, well, I'm married to a werewolf." She looked at their amused faces and amended her statement. "Or Lycan…whatever. By the way, what's the difference? Do you know?"

Elmira responded with a wide grin, "Yes, I know some differences. Lycans aren't controlled by the full moon, unlike the werewolf. They can shift any time they choose. There are pure Lycans, like your husband, but all werewolves have been transformed by a wolf's bite mixed with witchcraft. Lycans are smarter and somewhat stronger, and they can be royalty, as you are aware. Werewolves don't have royalty, and they aren't pack animals"—she wrung her hands—"I'm sure there are other differences, but those are the ones I know of."

"Hmm…interesting. Thank you for sharing the information," Julia commented. "It seems every day from here on out is going to be an adventure."

"But a marvelous one," Ofelia exclaimed. "You are unlike any other mortal woman. You were chosen by a powerful king."

"Yeah," she sighed, "I know, and I'm glad I'm with him. I've never known anyone like him." She started laughing hysterically. "Of course, that's pretty obvious, isn't it?"

Seth entered the caravan just then. "What's so funny?" he wondered.

Julia smiled at her handsome husband. "I'll tell you later. What did you and the others decide?"

He cocked his head curiously at her and replied, "Well, we decided to go hunting for now, and then we're going to sharpen our combat skills afterward."

She shot an amused grin at the other women. "I suppose that's manspeak for *we're going to wrestle and do some male bonding*." The ladies laughed with her.

"And you are correct," Seth chuckled. "We'll be hunting close by, but the Gypsy men will be here to guard the camp in our absence." He leaned down and kissed her tenderly. "I'll be back soon."

She nodded and looked at Elmira and Ofelia. "Lunch sounds like a splendid idea. Can I help you cook?"

Elmira smiled. "Sure! We'll teach you some authentic Romani recipes."

"Terrific. Let me just feed Ossy first." She looked around for her furry friend but didn't see him.

Ofelia pointed out the window. "He's playing with the children."

Julia looked outside and laughed at his antics. "He needs the exercise and loves the attention"—her face grew serious—"And, it seems, he can smell vampires, so I'll just leave him outside."

"Try not to worry. Our men are skillful fighters," Elmira assured her.

Seth and the others were careful to sniff the air for vampires while hunting their prey, but as he promised, they didn't stray too far. He decided to take a small hunting party out later, while leaving a couple men behind to help protect the camp. He couldn't begin to guess how many vampires were already in Armando's army, but if they were able to track even a few, it would work in their favor.

What do you call one dead vampire? A good start.

When they returned to camp, he was going to bite Yoska since the Gypsy still insisted he wanted to turn. Seth just wanted to feed first to keep his strength up. He was going to need it and soon. He could feel it in the air like an invisible electric energy, and it made his heart thump. *Something is coming.*

Armando, Zephryne, and the new vampire returned to Brad's house forty minutes later with two more people in tow.

"This is Jonah and Diana," Armando declared and pointed to the newcomers. "They didn't volunteer to join us, but I got my way regardless." He smiled vindictively at the shiny couple. "And, of course, you already know Craig. He was delicious, wasn't he, my pet?"

Melanie forced a smile and replied, "Yes, he was divine." She looked at the man she'd fed on earlier and felt sexual stirrings. He was big and burly—similar to Seth. She quickly looked away from him, though, so Armando wouldn't notice her lustful gaze. "Did you feed then?"

"Yes, we have all fed. One of our prey didn't make it, though." He opened his arms with a casual shrug. "I couldn't stop myself from draining her dry. She was just too satisfying to deny my thirst."

"I'm sure she was," Melanie mumbled.

Making casual conversation with him wasn't an easy task. He'd ended her mortal life when he took her as his bride, and she didn't think she would ever forgive him for it even if she lived for thousands of years or longer. *On the other hand, if I could spend that time with Seth...* She forced herself to remove him from her thoughts. He was forbidden fruit in every way imaginable. Craig, however, was a possibility worth examining.

"What now, my king?" Brad asked, sucking up as usual.

Armando paced the living room with his hands clasped behind him. "We'll continue to build our army as quickly as possible, and then we'll thin out the herd. We'll start with the Gypsies first, I imagine, just to piss off the Lycan king. Then we'll lie in wait for his retaliation."

Brad grinned. "The best defense is a good offense."

"Something like that," the vampire king growled. "For now, let's discuss how to take them down. I want to turn as many Gypsies as possible as opposed to just killing them. Their magic, combined with vampirism, will make them valuable assets—like my queen." He turned to address Melanie, reaching out and clasping her frigid hand. "We need to start tapping into your powers, my dear."

That was an appealing suggestion. "As you wish, Armando," she replied. Learning to use her magical gifts would only further her agenda.

"Brad, you can help us with that, and Zephryne can teach the newcomers to fight. They'll need to know the art of war to be successful against the Lycans." He shooed the other vampires away, so they retreated to Brad's basement.

Brad brought out the book of Rosci and black magic supplies to start with Melanie's first lesson. He chose to teach her how to curse someone, and the someone he had in mind was Julia.

Julia was helping the other women set the food on the table when a powerful chill made her body shake. Her head began to spin, and her vision blurred. She stumbled backward and collapsed to the ground before anyone could catch her.

"Julia! Are you all right?" Elmira screeched in panic and rushed to her side. "Can you hear me?" She touched Julia's face, telling Ofelia, "Her eyes are dilated, and her skin is cold."

Ofelia sprang into action by removing a protective charm she wore. "She needs this necklace. Someone might be practicing black magic against her," she exclaimed.

Elmira slipped the necklace around Julia's neck while Ofelia chanted a protection spell to undo the curse. Soon, Julia's eyes fluttered open, and she stared to focus on their concerned faces.

"What happened? Why am I on the ground?" she queried and slowly sat upright.

"It seems someone cursed you, but I've reversed it," Ofelia divulged. "You should be fine, but I want you to keep my blessed necklace on. The charm will protect you from future attempts."

Julia touched the crystal charm dangling from a black cord around her neck. It reflected the sun into tiny points of light on Ofelia's pretty face.

"Thank you. I'll be sure to take care of it," she replied.

"I have no doubt you will. Here, let me help you up," Ofelia offered with an extended hand.

Julia rose to her feet just as Seth and the others were heading in their direction. She gave her husband a weak smile in case he'd spotted her on the ground. She didn't want him to panic.

"What happened?" he demanded when he reached her. "Are you okay?"

She placed her hand on his shoulder, gazing into his amber-flecked eyes. "I'm fine; however, Ofelia thinks someone tried to curse me. She gave me her necklace to protect me, though. Wasn't that sweet of her?"

He tossed a glance at the Gypsy and nodded in her direction. "Thank you for looking out for my queen. Do you really think someone cursed her?" His voice came out high-pitched from a mixture of concern and anger.

Ofelia nodded. "It appears so, but as she told you, my necklace will protect her from future attempts. Whoever performed the curse will likely figure that out, though, and might try something else, so we need to be on the defensive. The best way to get to you—"

"Is to get to her," he interrupted and gawked at his wife. "I'm sorry I wasn't here to protect you. I won't leave you alone like that again."

She reached out and placed her palm against his face. "It's not your fault, and it was a curse, not a physical attack, so there was nothing you could've done to stop it or prevent it."

"I can prevent it," he growled. "I can destroy the dark Gypsy."

She knew he meant Brad, and it just made her think of Melanie again with a heavy heart. She pulled her phone out of her pocket and checked her voicemail, but it was empty.

"You're thinking about Melanie, aren't you?" he inquired. "Are you going to call her again?"

Julia looked up at him with sad eyes. "I'm beginning to think I should just call the police and file a missing person's report."

"Whatever you think is best," he replied and pulled her in for a hug.

"I still feel a little weak, so I'm going to eat, and then I'll go to the station," she noted and sat down with the others to dine.

After her first bite, her phone began to ring. She looked at the display and dropped her fork when she saw Melanie's name. "It's her!" she exclaimed before answering the call. "Melanie, is that you?"

Melanie's voice came through, but she sounded weak. "Hi, hon. I'm sorry I didn't return your calls. I went home to see my folks and ended up with a nasty case of the flu. I've been in bed for days," she explained. "I'm feeling a little better now, but I think I'm going to stay here a few more days."

"Oh, well, I'm sorry to hear you got sick. Did you call the bank and explain? I went by there today to look for you, and it seems your job is on the line," Julia informed her.

"Yeah, I called my boss and explained everything. She's fine with me taking a few extra days off. Are you doing okay? You sounded panicky in your messages."

Julia bit her lip. She couldn't go over everything with Melanie over the phone. "I'm fine. We'll catch up when you get home. Just do me one favor and stay away from Brad, okay?"

"Sure. I didn't care much for him anyway," Melanie responded and then said good-bye.

Julia summarized the call for Seth, who was sitting next to her even though he wasn't eating. "Well, at least you know she's okay, and you don't need to file a police report on her," he pointed out.

"I know, but there was something strange about her voice," Julia sighed.

He shrugged. "Maybe she's still sick."

Julia nodded. "Yeah, that's what she said. Oh well. I guess I'll find out more when she returns home." She shrugged it off and went back to her lunch.

Melanie scowled when she hung up. Julia sounded too normal to be hurt from the curse. She glared at Brad.

"How long does your curse take to go into effect?" she demanded. "She didn't sound hurt to me."

Brad rubbed his temples, and his mouth was in a tight line. "It should've worked immediately unless—"

"Unless what?" Melanie roared.

Brad swallowed hard because as upset as she was, Armando looked ready to boil over. "Unless she is with the Gypsies, and they stopped it with their magic."

"Damn it, Brad!" she swore. "We need something stronger that they can't undo."

Armando hissed, "I agree. What do you propose now?" He grabbed Brad by his shirt collar and yanked until they were nose to nose.

"We can try a voodoo doll, but if she's wearing a protective charm, it might not work. We need to get her alone, which we tried to do earlier, but she was gone from her home, and so were her belongings. We need to find her," he advised with a shaky voice. "Let me consult the tarot cards."

Armando shoved him away, causing him to fall to the floor. "Do it and don't let us down this time."

Seth led Yoska to the edge of the woods to change him, but he kept his sights on Julia. He was too far away for her to see them, but his keen eyesight allowed him to observe her in case anything else happened.

"So, how will this work? Is the change painful?" Yoska wondered.

Seth didn't lie to the man. "I have to bite you, so there will be pain from that. Then when you make your first shift, it will hurt since your limbs will be elongating. However, that pain will go away over time after your body gets used to transforming. There's still time to change your mind about this," he asserted.

Yoska took a deep breath and held his arm out for the bite. "No, I'm not afraid of pain. I was married once," he joked.

Seth laughed, but he found marriage to be a delight. "All right. I need to shift first," he replied and undressed.

Yoska's eyes went wide when he saw the huge creature, which had to be at least seven feet tall and had bulging muscles all over its body. Shaking, he undressed and extended his arm while squeezing his eyes shut in anticipation of the first wave of pain.

Razor-sharp burning pain tore through his arm like a bolt of lightning, and he yowled in agony. Then a new wave of hell washed over him as he felt his limbs and bones stretching to the point of feeling like he was being ripped in two. As the burning raged through his veins, he felt his jaw detaching from his face as it elongated into a muzzle full of knife-edged fangs. His fingers and toes followed suit as they stretched to excruciating lengths, and six-inch claws ripped through the tips.

His human screams turned into a fierce howling and snarling sound while the transformation completed. The insane hybrid of man and beast stood on its hind legs and slashed the air with its claws. It stared at Seth, who was still in his monstrous form, and snapped his slavering jaws, hungry for the tearing of flesh.

Seth jerked his head, so the other Lycan would follow him into the woods to hunt. He knew it was hungry for blood and meat. They ran side by side, chasing down two small deer herds and then burying their snapping jaws into the bucks' thick necks.

Forest animals scurried away as soon as they heard the ripping of flesh and smelled the blood-tinged air. Once their appetites were satiated, the Lycans traveled back toward the camp with blood and flesh dripping from their fangs.

The shift back to his mortal body still hurt Yoska, but it wasn't nearly as bad as the initial change. With a loud exhale, he re-dressed along with Seth.

"You endured the transformation well," Seth acknowledged.

Yoska rolled his brown eyes heavenward. "It was worse than I imagined it would be."

"Any regrets?" Seth inquired.

The other man shook his head. "No. I want to be effective in battle, and it's my best chance to be of help. Besides, you said it gets easier."

"I promise you that it does," Seth reaffirmed.

The Gypsy smiled. "It was nice to feel so powerful for once. I'll admit that."

Seth nodded. "Yes, it does feel good. Let's go back to camp. I need to check on my queen, and we need to get everyone together for combat practice."

"Does that mean I have to change back?" Yoska asked with a grimace.

Seth laughed at the man's sour expression. "No. We'll practice as humans, so no one gets injured. A lot of it is mental preparation anyway."

The women watched in amusement as the men rough-and-tumbled on the grass. It was easy to discern that some of it was just for fun, while other moves were specific maneuvers to have an advantage over the vampires. Seth informed everyone that the way to kill a vampire was by decapitation, so they incorporated knives and swords in their tactics.

"Fire is another way to kill one," Gerrant stated. "I've killed them in the past with it."

Seth arched a brow. "That is good to know. Thank you."

Using that information, he and the others cut down trees and carved multiple torches. Even some of the women helped with the carving.

"We need to locate more Lycans," Seth declared when they all sat down for a break. "I'm open to suggestions."

Ofelia stood up and spoke to her people. "We should scry for them," she suggested. "We have enough powerful magic within the council to make it work, especially if we use the Lycan king's pendant."

"I think that is a splendid suggestion," Elmira expressed, and the other council members nodded in agreement.

Seth, Julia, and the council members convened in the Council's caravan to give it a try while the others continued battle simulations. Seth handed the pendant of λύκος to Ofelia and sat on the sofa with Julia. They watched with great interest as the council members swung the necklace like a pendulum over a cup with tea leaves and a crystal ball.

Seth told the necklace, "Arată-ne secretele pe care le păstrezi. Dezvăluie-ne în cazul în care vârcolaci rula gratuit." *Show us the secrets you keep. Reveal to us where the Lycans run free.*

"I'm getting a vision from the leaves," Ofelia happily announced. "I can see a Lycan who is near." She sprinkled the leaves over the crystal ball to clarify her vision. "Modesto. He's in Modesto."

"That's about an hour-and-a-half from here," Julia chirped. "I can't believe our luck to find one so close."

Elmira cocked her head at Seth. "I think it's because the king is awake. Maybe some are migrating this way because they feel his pull," she conjectured.

Seth's brows furrowed. "I hope so because then maybe others are nearby."

"I'm not getting a clear picture of the king's destiny from the cards," Vonda, who was the eldest council member, complained. "Swing the necklace over it and try to get a reading, Ofelia."

Ofelia swung the pendant over the stacked deck and closed her eyes to concentrate. Then she flipped three cards: The Ace of Wands, The Fool, and Strength.

"The first card shows that you possess the energy, passion, and drive to impose your will. I believe this means you'll successfully build your army without resistance. The second card is The Fool. It represents new beginnings, optimism, and trust in life. I think it is referring to your marriage, saying that it will be a successful new beginning to your reign as king. The final card is Strength, and it is about courage, power, and the integration of animal self. I think that, given who you are, it is self-explanatory"—she stacked the cards back together—"All in all, your reading shows you will be successful in your endeavors, and you'll have the love and respect of your clan," she divulged.

Elmira had been swirling the leaves again, and she smiled broadly. "I think I see another Lycan tribe." She sprinkled the leaves over the crystal ball and waved her hand over it. "I do. I can see a small group of Lycans in Reno, Nevada."

Julia typed on her phone and declared, "That's three-and-a-half hours away."

Elmira stared at Seth with narrowed eyes.

"What's wrong? What are you thinking?" he asked her.

She relaxed her face into a slight smile. "I'm just wondering if you can use your pendant and the crystal ball to create a portal to send a message to the other Lycans we've found. That way they can come to you instead of us going to find them. Perhaps you can link your minds."

Seth sighed, "I suppose it's worth a shot."

He rose from the sofa and reclaimed his necklace. He held it over the crystal ball and closed his eyes to concentrate. When he opened them again, he could see the lone Lycan in Modesto. He concentrated on the man, trying to tap into his thoughts, and it appeared to work because the man's head snapped up from what he was doing in his home, and he looked all around him.

"I think he feels my presence," Seth whispered but maintained his focus.

"Good. Tell him with your mind to come to you," Elmira responded just as quietly.

Seth mentally told the man who he was and that he was building an army to defeat the vampires. He told the man to travel to San Francisco. At first, he didn't think it worked, but then the man nodded in understanding.

"I think he heard me, so I'm going to try it with the others," Seth announced.

He concentrated on the small tribe in Fresno until the vision became clear in the crystal ball. Then he repeated the process. There were five Lycans in the tribe, and they all seemed to hear him, and just like the other one had, they nodded in understanding.

"It worked. I felt myself connected with the five men, and they understood me," he told the group with pride. "This makes the process so much easier."

Julia smiled with relief. "So, what now?"

"We try to find more."

Brad consulted the cards as promised, but the reading didn't provide him with a clear direction of where Julia had gone. What it provided was a glum outlook for King Armando, but he kept that information to himself.

"What does your reading say?" Armando queried.

Brad quickly responded, "It's not entirely clear, so I'm going to scry for her instead."

Armando glared at the Gypsy. "Why didn't you do that in the first place?" he demanded. "Why are you wasting time with tarot cards?"

Brad hunched his shoulders and looked down at his feet. "I'm sorry, but I was hoping to see what the future had in store for her too."

"And?" Irritation laced the king's voice.

"Like I said, the reading wasn't clear. It came out conflicted," Brad lied.

Armando narrowed his eyes on the man, trying to read his expression. "Carry on. I want you to locate her for me."

Brad bowed his head in subservience and pulled a map and scrying crystal out of his desk drawer. He tapped into his power and swung the pendant over the map until the crystal was finally pulled down to a specific location.

"She's in Chinatown," he announced with relief. He was sure he wouldn't have survived another failure. "The Gypsy camp is in Chinatown."

Armando rubbed his chin. "So, they are camping with the Gypsy clan then. That's a smart move on the Lycan's part, but it won't dissuade us. Or, rather, it won't dissuade *you*. Find a way to get to her," he ordered, spun on his heel, and left Brad frozen in place.

Brad stared after him, clenching his hands into tight fists. *How am I supposed to manage that?* He walked to his cabinets and rifled through them, looking for anything and everything that might help. He pulled out potion bottles, charms, pendants, and spell books. He also grabbed the tarot cards again and his crystal ball. If there was ever a time to tap into his dark magic, it was right then.

Melanie sat in a large chair, watching the spectacle. Brad was rushing around to grab as much black magic paraphernalia as he could, spreading it out on the dining room table. Beads of sweat ran down his face as he frantically flipped through book after book.

"Do you have any idea what you're looking for?" she taunted.

His eyes became slits, and he snapped, "I'm looking for anything and everything that will help us."

"*Us* or you?" she cackled.

He turned his back on her without answering, but his heavy breathing let her know that she'd pissed him off.

"Are you going to help me or just sit there on your ass and judge?" he finally ranted.

She languidly rose from the chair and meandered to his side. "I'll help. You just haven't asked for it yet. What do you want me to do?"

He looked up from the book he was flipping through. "Start looking through the books for any spells that will help us get Julia."

She cocked her head at him. "Such as an abduction spell? Does such a thing even exist?"

"I doubt it," he scoffed. "However, there is a spell to bend someone's will; although, I need rain water to carry it out, and it's not supposed to rain for two days yet."

Melanie tapped a page in the book she was looking at and told him, "I want to try this one. It's a marriage curse."

He thrummed his fingers on the table while mulling it over. That would work in his favor too, but there was one large problem. "Their marriage was part of the prophecy. Divine marriages can't be cursed. Sorry."

He pulled a candle lighter out of a drawer and began lighting his assorted candles.

"Why are you doing that?" she wondered.

He sighed, "I'm lighting them for their relevance. Purple improves magical abilities and is for success, fortune telling, and prophecy. The gold candle is for victory, strength, and courage. The yellow candle provides confidence in spell casting, and the blue is for wisdom, truth, and luck."

She looked skeptical. "Well, that remains to be seen."

"Oh, ye of little faith," he mocked. "This is only the beginning."

He went back to his set of drawers and removed a mirror, a sheet of black paper, and a picture that she couldn't make out until he laid it on the table. It was a photo of Julia sleeping. The black paper had a few strands of hair taped to it.

"Is that what I think it is?" she inquired.

He smiled smugly to himself. "It's her hair that she left on my pillow."

Her jaw went slack. "Your pillow? Did you screw her and when?"

He puffed his chest out and chuckled. "Yes, and it was a few days ago."

"But she was with Seth, so how did you make that happen?" She didn't care that he'd slept with her friend; she just wanted to know how she could use his tricks to sleep with Seth.

His grin was malicious, and an evil twinkle graced his eyes. "I might have slipped her an elixir that made her vulnerable to my *charms*."

Melanie's eyes bulged, but her lip curled upward. "You slipped her a roofie?"

"No. I used black magic to make a tonic for her morning coffee. I suppose it has a similar effect, though," he replied.

She pointed to the mirror on the table. "What's that for?"

"We can use mirrors like crystal balls to look in on the enemy, and we can also use them as a way to see in the immediate future; however, that isn't always reliable, so I avoid it. It can be used to place a hex too," he explained. "Right now, I want to see her."

He flipped through the book in front of him until he found what he sought. While she looked in the mirror, he chanted something in a foreign language, but nothing happened. Only her reflection stared back at her.

"I don't see anything," she said in a bored tone.

He looked frustrated. "Shit! I think the camp has a protective shield or something."

"So now what?" she asked with a yawn.

His look of frustration was replaced by one of determination. "Now we perform a black magic attack."

The sun was going down, and Seth still wanted to search the woods for vampires before the camp settled in for the night. He also planned to take shifts with the others for keeping watch all night—the time when vampires were the most active. He was glad to have Oscar there, too, to help alert them if he smelled their stench.

After their final combat practice for the day, two more Gypsy men requested to be turned. Thus, while the others guarded the camp, Seth took Jared and Marcus into the woods and bit them. He would have waited until morning, but they were eager, and he needed to build his army as quickly as possible.

When they were finished with the agonizing transformation, Seth went back into camp and summoned Rahl and Gerrant. He knew they were also purebreds, which made them strong like him.

"We need to search the woods for vampires. I'll leave Yoska, Jared, Marcus, and Aric at the camp for protection. Lobo and Brody will come with us. I think I know where the vampires are hiding out, but I'd rather wait until we have a larger army to attack them there," he announced.

A booming voice suddenly rang out from behind him, and all heads turned. "Are you the king?" a large man inquired as he approached with a tall woman.

Seth recognized him from the crystal ball. "I am King Seth, and I recognize you from my vision earlier today."

"Yes, you contacted me. I'm Caleb, and this is my woman, Kali," he remarked and gestured to the female. "We came here from Modesto, and we are both purebred Lycans. I heard your conversation, and as an experienced vampire slayer, I'd like to hunt them with you. It will give me the chance to prove myself worthy of your army."

Kali chimed in, "I'm also an experienced warrior, so I will stay behind to guard your camp."

"All right," Seth conceded. "Let's gather the others and get to it."

After everyone assembled, he introduced the newcomers to the camp. Yoska, Jared, and Marcus were shifted, per his instructions, and placed on guard. He told them to stay that way in case of an attack because shifting through the pain again would take too long.

"You'll be able to smell the vampires if they get close, so be on the alert for a sickly metallic odor," he advised. "And don't worry about remaining shifted. Soon, you'll be able to turn within a matter of seconds. Soon, it won't hurt anymore." He gestured to the hunting party, and they headed to the woods.

Two miles out from the camp, they stumbled across two bloodsuckers. Seth could tell the vampires had recently been turned because their offensive odor wasn't as predominant as usual, and their inexperience made them easy to dispatch. They were quickly beheaded and disposed of in the thick underbrush.

The Lycans continued traipsing through the trees until Seth gestured for them to follow him back. Once he had enough soldiers, they'd hunt near the vampires' turf— Brad's house.

April 17, 2014

ꙅThe morning sun streamed through the window and landed squarely on Seth's stubble-covered face. He looked at Julia, who was nestled up against him, and began to play with her silky golden hair.

Julia's eyes fluttered open and found Seth staring at her. "Good morning," she sighed and glanced at the alarm clock. "It's only 7:00, so you should go back to sleep. You were up late."

"I'm not tired anymore. I'm wide awake," he assured her with a suggestive grin.

She smiled back at him. "Well, I should take advantage of that then," she drawled and ran her fingers down his body underneath the blanket.

She clasped her hand around his hardened shaft and squeezed, moving it slowly up and down. His guttural growl urged her to pick up the tempo.

"I want you," he cried out before climbing on top of her.

"Take me," she replied in a voice that was just as husky as his. She spread her thighs to receive him. She was aching and ready for him.

He teased her entrance first, rubbing without entering. He could feel the heat radiating from her velvety softness, begging him to get closer. He pushed gently until he was inside her forge, his erection filling her, stripping away everything but her aching need. They began to move together as one, their panting thick with desire. He pulled out almost all the way, then plunged deep.

She moved under him, moaning as he filled her and meeting his driving rhythm beat for beat. Arching her hips, she met him thrust for thrust. Rapture washed over her body in tidal waves as he gave her what she wanted.

Seth stared into her eyes as he devoured her body with his devout passion. When she moaned his name, his tempo increased to bring her to another powerful climax, and her insides hugged him as she tumbled over into a chasm of ecstasy. Feeling the need to join her, he clasped her hips, pulling her hard into his final thrust. His release spilled into her hot center while his mouth worked over hers.

"I love you," he whispered huskily against her lips.

Julia was quick to reply with her confession of love. "I love you too, and you should know that I haven't said that to a man since I was a teenager."

He stared into her eyes and ran his finger down her cheek and neck. "Someone must have hurt you to close you off to love for that long, but don't worry because I'm going to put the broken pieces back together."

Oscar interrupted their tender moment with a loud whimper. "I think someone needs to potty," she stated. "I'll take him."

Seth didn't let her climb out of bed, though. "No, you deserve to be pampered by your king, so if you want to take a shower, go ahead. I'll take our son for a walk," he told her with a grin.

"Our son?" she chuckled while climbing out of bed.

Seth pulled his clothes on. "Well, yeah, he's family. Aren't you, big boy?" he cooed to the dog.

Still laughing, she dressed and went to the utility block for the women to relieve herself and take a shower. She had been initially surprised that the Gypsy clan didn't have bathrooms in the caravans for convenience, but they'd explained to her that bathrooms in the home were considered *mochadi*, meaning unclean. She shrugged it off without a fuss, though. She didn't have to share their beliefs or completely adapt to their culture because they were only there as guests.

After her shower, she helped the women prepare breakfast for the camp while Seth gathered with the men. Everyone stopped what they were doing, however, when a group of five men and three women approached.

Seth recognized the men from his second vision. "Welcome. I'm King Seth, and I'm pleased that you received my message and came to join us. Please introduce yourselves," he loudly announced, so everyone could hear him.

A bearded man with black hair stepped forward. "I am Marric, a purebred and leader of our group. This is Mei, my wife, and she is also a purebred," he claimed.

Another couple stepped forward, and the man said, "I'm Deryn, and this is my woman, Gabriella. We are both hybrids."

The third coupled followed. "I'm Wyatt, and this is my wife, Sage. I'm a purebred, but she is mortal."

Two men stepped forward, and the taller one introduced them both. "I'm Landon, and I'm a purebred. He's Mason, and he's a hybrid."

Seth looked them over with a smile. His army was shaping up nicely. "Thank you all for coming to join us in the fight against the vampire king," he remarked. "I think we are now large enough in number to plan our attack."

Marric looked over the crowd. "How many Lycans are we in total, my king?"

"If we include the women, we are eighteen in number. I'm assuming, of course, that the women are willing to battle alongside us."

"We are," Mei proudly declared.

Kali walked up next to the other Lycan women. "I am too."

"I want to help as well. I'm ready to be turned," Halley, one of the Gypsies, called out.

Seth was surprised to have one of the women volunteer. In his time, the females only volunteered to shift in order to make better mates for the Lycan men and bear strong children. However, he had no intentions of turning Julia. He couldn't stand the idea of her going through the pain of shifting.

"If you're certain you want to, I'll change you unless the king would rather do it," Landon volunteered.

Seth nodded at the other Lycan. "That's fine with me. Go ahead and do it now if she's ready."

"Wait!" Elmira called out to stop them from walking off. "Drink this first. It has something in it to help you survive the pain." She thrust a cup toward Halley who quickly downed it. "Give it a minute to kick in before you proceed," Elmira pleaded.

"I will," the young woman promised.

Seth addressed the others. "I want us to run through tactics again, but let's have our meal first."

The entire camp, including the newcomers, sat down to a hearty breakfast and enjoyed another normal morning before all hell broke loose.

Armando woke up in a foul mood. Two of his newborn soldiers hadn't come back to the dwelling after they went out hunting the night before. That either meant they were going rogue or the Lycans had found them.

"Zephryne, come here," he bellowed at the top of the stairs to the basement, and she immediately obeyed.

"What is it, King Armando?" she softly asked. She could sense his bad mood.

He paced the living room while she knelt before him. "I want you to take a small group to search the woods for the missing newborns. While you're at it, turn everyone you see, and of course, you're to kill every Lycan you cross paths with."

"Yes, my king. We'll leave immediately," she acquiesced.

Armando then summoned Melanie and Brad. "What are you doing to get that wench in our hands?" he demanded.

Brad answered on their behalf, "We are going to perform what is called a black magic attack on her and the Gypsy camp. Also, I thought about stealing blood from a local blood bank, so you can use it to feed the ones you want to turn, and it will keep them satiated when they aren't hunting. It won't taste as fresh, but it should make do."

"A blood bank, huh? How intriguing," the king mumbled. "Yes, do get us a large supply. Melanie will go with you to help"—he looked at his wife—"Turn every human you come into contact with, darling queen."

She bowed her head. "As you desire."

Armando turned toward the front door. "I'm going hunting, and I suggest you do the same before you venture out," he commented to Melanie and left.

"I'll start the magical attack while you hunt," Brad suggested to her. "I'm anxious to see if it works."

She nodded and left the house to find her prey. Brad's blood would have to make do to complete the transformation when she carried her weakened prey back to the house until they robbed the blood bank.

Glad to finally be alone, Brad got to work. Before working on the black magic attack, he performed some spells that would solely benefit him. He cast two protection spells along with a spell to strengthen his Black Dragon amulet. He'd never used the spells before, so he couldn't attest to their effectiveness, but it was worth a try. He wouldn't be able to withstand Armando's wrath without help.

Once he was ready for the magical attack, he got out the necessary supplies. He retrieved the strands of Julia's hair, the photograph of her, and a voodoo doll he'd secretly been working on. His initial goal was to inflict sickness on her, making her come to him to reverse it.

He closed his eyes to concentrate on her aura while holding her photograph. He used his mind's eye to see what protective measures she was using. Unlike before with the mirror, he was able to see her this time. If she'd been using a protective charm or amulet previously, she wasn't currently wearing it. Since he was able to tap into her, he decided to inflict a mental attack. It would make her obey his commands, much like the bending someone's will spell he'd wanted to use. It would be better than making her ill.

He opened his eyes and studied the voodoo doll. He pulled the strands of hair off the paper and splayed them across the doll and then pinned her photo to it.

He closed his eyes to see her face again. She was eating breakfast and smiling at someone—probably her fleabag husband. He squeezed the doll's right hand to see if it had an effect on her. Then he happily watched her drop her fork and grab her hand with the other. She began to massage it. *It's working!*

He let go of the doll's hand and soothed it by stroking its head. Correspondingly, Julia's hand flew to her scalp while a look of confusion crossed her pretty face. It was time to make her bend to his will.

He whispered into the doll's ear, "You want something from your apartment. Go home *alone.* Do it now."

He saw her get up from her seat, giving him ten minutes to get to her place to lie in wait for her. He quickly cleaned up the mess, tucked the doll into his pocket, and left before Armando and Melanie returned.

Julia had the sudden urge to go home. She needed *something*. "I'm going to quickly run back to the apartment. I forgot something when we packed," she told Seth.

"What is it? I can get it for you," he offered.

She felt her face grow warm. "I'm not sure what it is. I just have the strong feeling that I forgot something. But, I need to check on the place and drop off next month's rent check anyway," she informed him.

"Well, I'll go with you. They can keep practicing simulations without me." He looked over at the men and women who were already sharpening their battle skills. Halley had been turned and was practicing too.

Julia scuffed at loose dirt with the toe of her shoe. "Don't take this the wrong way, but I'd rather go alone. I need a few minutes to myself," she said quietly. "I think I'll check on Melanie again, and I might call my parents. I have to let them know about you yet."

His face fell. "Okay, if you're sure. Get back soon." He gave her a quick kiss and then trotted off to practice with the others.

Brad anxiously watched the street from her kitchen window. He'd picked her lock to slip inside, and he couldn't wait to see the look of surprise on her face when she saw him.

Her yellow car was easy to spot speeding down the street, so he ran to the bedroom and hid behind the door, hoping she came alone as he'd instructed. He tensed up when he finally heard her come in through the front door. His fists were clenching into tight balls, turning his knuckles white, and his breathing was shallow.

Then he heard her coming down the hallway, so he got ready to pounce. She entered the bedroom, alone, and began looking through her dresser with her back to him.

He stepped out from behind the door and slammed it shut.

Julia spun around with a shriek. "Brad! What the hell are you doing here, and how did you get in?" she demanded. Her eyes darted around the room, looking for an escape route and a weapon, but she couldn't find either.

Brad approached her with an evil laugh. "I'm so glad to see you again, Julia. Aren't you just as happy to see me? Reunions shouldn't be tense."

Julia tried to back up but hit the wall. "What do you want?" she asked, her voice trembling.

He cocked his head and smiled. "I want what I've always wanted—you." He held up a zip tie and advanced toward her.

Julia tried to bolt past him, but he pulled the voodoo doll out of his pocket and pressed hard into its leg, causing her to fall to the floor.

"Tsk-tsk. That's no way to say hello," he grunted and jerked her upright.

Julia tried to take a swing at him, but it felt like someone was pinning her arms. She noticed the voodoo doll then, and he was pinching the arms to its sides.

"What the hell is that?" she squawked with her eyes opened wide.

"It's my replica of you," he replied with smug satisfaction while he put the zip tie around her wrists, pulling it tight.

"What are you going to do with me?" she cried as tears streamed down her cheeks.

He leaned in and forced his mouth on hers before telling her, "I'm taking you to meet a king."

Seth was sharpening his combat skills with the others when a sharp pain tore through him, and the pendant of λύκος began to glow. He sniffed the air while scanning the grounds and surrounding trees for vampires, but there weren't any in the area. Then panic filled him as Julia ran through his mind. *She's in danger!*

Ofelia called out his name just as he made his conclusion. "I think there's something wrong with your queen. I want to check on her, but I can't get a vision."

His eyes widened more, and his nostrils flared. "I got that feeling too. I'm going to go after her," he exclaimed and began tearing off his clothes. There was no time for modesty.

She thrust an amulet toward him. "I found her protective necklace in the showers. She needs to have it back on. It will ward off the dark magic and the evil eye."

Seth put it on and shifted without saying anything to the others, but they sensed his panic, so they all shifted too. Lobo, Brody, Rahl, and Aric stayed in the camp to protect it, while the other fourteen ran after their king.

Seth's heart beat in his ears while his clawed feet thundered on the ground. He heard the others running behind him, but he didn't look back. It was good to know they were there, though, because he didn't know what to expect when he got to the apartment.

He finally reached the building and paused long enough to smell the air. He couldn't smell vampire stench, but he did recognize Brad's odor. The others had caught up to him and stared at him for a command. Since they were unified as one pack, he could project his thoughts to them.

Wait here. I'm going inside.

Hoping no one saw him, he climbed up the trellis outside the bedroom window. He could still smell the vampire stench on it from the one he'd killed prior to the blood moon. He broke the glass and shifted back to human form to wedge his way inside. Then he ran naked through the apartment to find her. He saw evidence of a struggle in the bedroom, and a few droplets of blood were on the carpet.

He leapt back through the window, shifting mid-air, and took off running with the others close on his heels. He ran as quickly as he could toward Brad's cabin in the woods.

Julia came to with a pounding headache and a sore jaw. Her wrists were bound, and she was in the back of Brad's car. He'd struck her across the face when she tried to get away, and her eye socket still felt ready to explode as her cheek pulsed from the bruise. She struggled to sit up, and it caught his attention, making him look at her in the rearview mirror. He wore a smug grin that she wanted to cut off his face.

"Hello again. I hope you're ready to behave yourself because I hate having to hit a woman," he remarked. "You know, your new husband isn't doing a very good job at protecting you. I think I could do much better."

"He's going to kill you!" she spat.

He wagged a finger at her. "Tsk-tsk. Don't make me slap you again for being vindictive. Unless, of course, you want a matching set of bruises."

"Fuck you!" she screamed as loud as she could while trying to get her hands loose. It was to no avail, though. He'd tied the zip tie too tight; there wasn't any wiggle room.

"Oh my," he feigned shock. "That's no way for a queen to speak. Do you kiss your Lycan with that mouth?"

Julia's teeth ground together from rage, and she kicked his seat as hard as she could. Luckily, she had strong legs, so it thrust him forward, and he lost control of the car which spun off the winding road and into a large tree. He slammed into the steering wheel while she flew into the back of his seat.

Desperate to escape, she ignored the massive shooting pain coursing through her body and opened the door, tumbling out to the ground. Brad was out cold, so she scrambled away from the car and helped herself to her feet before he came to. She'd heard him breathing, so she knew he was still alive.

She stumbled through the underbrush, falling twice, trying to find a way to her freedom. The hill was too steep and treacherous to climb up to the highway with her hands bound, so she ran aimlessly through the trees to find a level area.

Tears poured down her face, and she mentally called out to her husband. *Seth, I need you!* Coincidence or not, a loud howl rang through the trees, and for once, it was comforting.

"Seth!" she bellowed. "Seth, I need you! Please come find me!"

A loud rustling in the trees made her stop running and look around. She hoped with all her heart it was her husband and not Brad, but it was someone she never expected—Melanie.

Julia felt a mixture of relief and confusion when she saw her best friend. "Melanie, I'm so glad to see you! Brad abducted me, so we have to get out of here. He's crazy, and he's the serial killer the police are looking for," she cried.

Melanie didn't seem at all surprised. She just slowly advanced with a catty grin, and the look in her eyes worried Julia. She looked almost hostile.

"Mel, what's wrong? Let's get out of here!" she screeched while mentally praying Seth heard her cries and would burst through the trees.

Melanie chuckled low in her throat. Then she parted her lips and smiled to show off her fangs while still making her stealthy approach. Julia tried to back away, but shock overwhelmed her, freezing her in place like a giant cement block.

"Did you know that Brad is my cousin?" Melanie asked when she stopped directly in front of Julia. "Yeah, I was surprised too"—she reached out and stroked a strand of Julia's hair—"but don't worry because I didn't sleep with him. I know you did, though."

Julia finally found her strength to move, and she started backing away. "That was a mistake. I didn't intentionally do that. I was sick that day, and I wasn't aware of what was happening," she explained. "Who did this to you, Mel? Who turned you into a...a...a..."

"Vampire? Is that the word you're looking for?" Melanie purred. "I'm the queen of the vampires, you know? King Armando gave me his immortal kiss, and here we are at last. I've been looking for you, and I'm hungry."

Seth heard his queen's cry for help, and he thrashed through the trees to get to her. It was difficult to pick up her scent while he was running, though, so he had to come to a stop. He communicated with the others.

Spread out and find my queen!

The others swiftly obeyed, running in all directions. Seth kept heading northwest where her fragrance seemed to be coming from. Then another odor hit him. It was the despicable scent of vampire.

His heart felt like it was about to explode while he bolted through the woods. The stench was growing stronger, though, so he knew he was on the right path. He let the others know, hoping they were close enough to hear him.

This way. Head northwest.

He let out a piercing howl to let her and the vampire know that he was on his way, and he was getting close.

Brad regained consciousness, and his body was throbbing all over. "You bitch!" he screamed and turned around to hit her, but she was gone. "Fuck!"

He struggled to get the door open because it was mashed in from the accident. When he finally did, he stumbled out and scanned the area for her. He hoped that she was also injured and, therefore, didn't get too far. He limped through the trees where the grass appeared to be trampled down. A loud howl made him freeze in his tracks, however, and he looked all around trying to figure out which direction it came from. Other howls followed, and he could tell there was more than one Lycan in the woods.

Frightened, he climbed the steep, rocky hill to get back to the road. The rocks cut into his hands as he tried to maintain his grip, but it was better than the slash of a Lycan's claws, so he dealt with it. He doubted the creatures would chase him on the highway. They weren't stupid enough to risk exposure.

He finally made it to the road and began his trek toward his cabin. There, he'd have some reinforcements, and he could also try a spell or two to deter the Lycans. As he fought through the pain, he picked up his pace, hoping someone would drive by and offer him a lift. He still had a mile to go before he'd reach home.

He heard a car coming, so he turned and waved the driver down. The man pulled up to him and rolled down his window.

"Are you okay?" the man asked, looking at the blood stains on Brad's shirt from his cuts and scrapes.

"I was in an accident back there and could use a lift to my house. I live only a mile up the road, and I'll pay you for the gas."

The man smiled and gestured for him to get into the car. "You don't have to pay me. Hell, I'm headed that direction anyway."

Brad climbed inside and told the man, "I live off a gravel road, so you'll need to turn there. I'd try to hike it, but my legs are really hurting from the accident."

"How did you go off the road? I think I saw your car back there," the man replied.

Brad lied, "A damn deer ran out in front of me again. This is the first time it ever caused me damage, though."

"It was probably running from that crazy howling I heard. Are wolves common in these woods? I'm just visiting my daughter out here. I'm actually from Nevada," the driver responded.

Sorry, but you won't be seeing your daughter today. I've got too many damn vampires to feed.

"Unfortunately, they've been migrating here lately," Brad answered. "They're a real nuisance."

His gravel drive came into view, so he pointed it out, and the driver eased into the turn.

"I appreciate the lift, and I'd like to pay you for your trouble," Brad commented when the car came to a stop in front of his house.

"Nah, we're good," the guy grumbled.

Brad turned to him and replied, "I wish that were true," and then he stabbed the man in the gut. He'd seen Armando staring out the window, so at least one thirsty vampire was home, and if he didn't want to feed, they could drain the man's blood into a pitcher and store it. *Blech.*

Once he got the body inside, he'd take the man's car to the blood bank for the rest of the supplies. He didn't want to stick around, working on curses for the Lycans, because Armando would, no doubt, have questions about Julia. He wasn't in the mood to have his head ripped off—literally.

Both women heard the howling. "Do you hear that? That's my husband coming for me," Julia announced, feeling hopeful. "That, of course, means he's also coming for you." She tried to make her tone threatening, but she was terrified. Melanie could still attack her before Seth got there. She opened her mouth to scream out to him, but Melanie pounced and covered it with her clammy hand.

"It's okay because I have a plan," Melanie growled and then sank her fangs into Julia's throat. She was only a few slurps in, though, when she had to drop her prey and run for her life because she smelled the strong odor of Lycan.

Julia lay crumpled on the ground, clasping her hand to her punctured throat and moaning. A sudden rustling in the trees made her insides quake as she considered the possibility of Melanie returning or another vampire. A sudden low growl made her pulse quicken, however. She blinked her tear-filled eyes as Seth burst through the thick trees. She knew it was him because he was wearing his pendant of λύκος.

He ran to her and knelt, cradling her in his arms. Tears ran down his muzzle, but when he saw the bite wound, he growled and let out an ear-piercing howl. Three members of his new clan rushed to his side and saw the mark too. He looked at them and relayed his thoughts.

Hunt the vampire who did this. Bring me their head.

The three Lycans took off in a run in separate directions while Seth scooped Julia up and bolted for the camp. With all the magic there, they should be able to save his queen. They'd better.

Seth rushed to Ofelia and Elmira, who were staring with gaping mouths. He lay Julia on the grass and pointed his claw to her bite wound before using the sharp nail to cut the zip tie. Then, once again ignoring modesty, he shifted to his human body.

"What can we do? Save her," he bellowed.

"The necklace. Put the amulet back on her," Ofelia advised, and he pulled it off over his head, quickly putting it over his wife's.

Julia's breathing was shallow and ragged, and her skin was extremely pale and clammy.

"Carry her to your caravan," Elmira commanded, and he quickly sprang into action. Ofelia followed, but Elmira went in another direction.

Seth lay Julia on the bed and stepped aside, so Ofelia could work her magic. He was at a loss when it came to helping his queen, and it just made his rage burn hotter. Ofelia clutched her pendant with one hand and placed the other over the bite. Then she chanted a healing spell in Romani.

The door opened, and Elmira barged in with a bowl of water in one hand and some amulets and talismans in the other.

"This is an herbal healing water to wash away the demonic residue," she proclaimed and handed the wet cloth from the bowl to Ofelia who pressed it to the bite.

The women held hands, and Elmira clutched the pendant she wore after placing the others on Julia's chest. Together, the women chanted spells for healing and for purging demons. Ofelia parted Julia's lips to check for fangs.

"Her teeth are normal, so she hasn't fed yet," she commented.

"I knew that because I would've smelled it on her," Seth rumbled. His nerves had his temper on edge.

Julia's eyes slowly fluttered open, and she looked at their faces in confusion. "Am I back in the camp? What happened?" she asked softly.

"You're fine, my darling, and you're safe with us. Do you remember anything?" Seth reached for her hand and pressed it gently between his.

Julia wet her lips and thought. Then her eyes widened as visions of Melanie flooded her brain. "Melanie is a vampire now! In fact, she said she's the queen"—she stared into Seth's worried face—"She was going to kill me, but then we heard you. She bit me, though." Her hand went to the cloth that was still pressed to her wound.

"It's okay, my love. She didn't drink enough to cause you permanent harm," Seth soothed her. "And the ladies here have used their powers to help you." He nodded at Ofelia and Elmira.

Julia didn't look comforted though. She ran her tongue over her teeth, but they didn't feel out of the ordinary. "Am I going to turn into a vampire?"

Elmira chuckled, "No, Queen Julia. You have to drink a mortal's blood to convert."

Julia made a sour face. "Well, then I have nothing to worry about because I'm never doing that."

Seth dressed and climbed into the bed beside her, pulling her into his snug embrace.

Elmira addressed them, "Well, I think she'll be weak but otherwise fine. We'll let you rest now. If you need anything, just yell for us."

"Please tell the Lycans to stay on duty. I'm sure this isn't the only attack they have planned," Seth told her with a dire tone. "I'll be out there in a little while to continue our simulations."

She bowed her head. "As you wish, my king." She walked out the door behind Ofelia.

"I was so scared," Julia admitted to him. "I was scared you wouldn't get there in time."

He squeezed her tighter. "Oh, I was too, darling. I was petrified as we scoured the forest for you." He paused to kiss her forehead. "I sent the others after her, so hopefully, they'll find the witch and destroy her."

Julia recalled something Melanie had told her. "She said Brad is her cousin. Isn't that strange?"

He connected the dots. "If she's his cousin, then she must be a dark Gypsy too, and that's why she was chosen to be Armando's queen. We'll have to be extra cautious because that's a lot of dark magic in one being. I need to warn the others."

"Go ahead and tell them now. I'm just going to sleep for a while," she mumbled. "I'll be all right by myself."

Oscar whimpered outside the caravan door, so Seth let him in. "You're not alone. Someone is worried about you," he chuckled as the dog jumped into the bed with her. "Now, you protect Mommy while Daddy goes to work." He patted Oscar on the head and gave Julia a soft kiss. "I'll check on you soon."

"Okay, but try to keep your clothes on this time," she teased. "No need to make the other fellas jealous."

"I'll try," he promised, gave her another kiss, and then ran off to practice.

Julia closed her eyes and drifted off to sleep, but she was plagued by horrifying vampire dreams.

Melanie climbed the giant trees and leapt between them to avoid the Lycans. It took several minutes to reach her safe haven, and she was out of breath when she finally did.

Armando was waiting for her. "What took you so long, and who is that I smell on you?" he demanded.

Melanie knew if she told him the truth, she might suffer consequences, so she made up a story. "She was a sweet young hiker that had the misfortune of trekking in my direction," she purred. "Where's my cousin?" she asked to change the subject.

"He said he was going to the blood bank to grab us a healthy supply. It won't make do for me, but perhaps it will pacify your and the newborns' palates," he stated while pacing a circle around her. "I must admit that young hiker smells tasty. Was she good?"

Melanie licked her fangs and didn't have to lie. "She was positively scrumptious."

"Where is she? I told you to turn more soldiers," he grumbled and gave her a hard look.

She truthfully replied, "I smelled Lycans nearby and heard them howling. There was more than one, so I thought it best to leave her and run for it."

He nodded with a sigh. "I see. I suppose you had no choice then. Next time, we'll hunt together."

Brad, thankfully, came in through the front door, carrying a cardboard box full of bags of blood. He took them to the refrigerator and piled them in.

"The blood will stay fresher when refrigerated," he explained when he reentered the room. "I suppose you can set them out to get the blood to room temperature before consumption."

Armando made a sour face. "Blech. I'll keep seeking warm bodies but thank you. The newborns can have at it."

Zephryne crashed through the door along with Craig, Jonah, Diana, and four newbies who looked unconscious and had to be carried.

"Brad, we need your blood before we lose them," Zephryne demanded with a scowl.

Brad went back to the kitchen and then reappeared with four of the bags. "Here you go. Feed them this."

She made a disgusted face at the bagged blood and glanced at Armando. "Is that okay with you, my king?"

He answered with a simple nod, so she passed the bags to the other lucid vampires, and they fed the contents to the newborns. Once they were satiated and feeling better, Armando sent all of them out hunting for more soldiers.

"Bring back as many as you can. We're going to need them soon," he instructed. "You can take some of the blood with you to complete the transformations wherever you are."

Zephryne bowed her head. "As you desire, my king."

After they left, he pulled Brad aside. "What about the Lycan's queen? Have you made any progress at all?" he inquired with a threatening tone.

Brad tried to think of a quick lie. "I had the little bitch, but a deer ran across the road and made me wreck my car, so she got away while I was unconscious."

The vampire king grabbed him by the throat and held him suspended mid-air. "You seem to have misunderstood my instructions before. You are to get her and bring her to me without incident. I don't want your excuses anymore, or it will be your head."

Brad couldn't answer, so only strangled pleas came out while his arms and legs flailed. Armando finally dropped him into a heap on the floor, and he took painful gulps of air into his burning lungs.

"Do whatever you need to do to get me that girl and do it now," Armando thundered.

Brad scrambled to his feet and backed away from the angry vampire. "Yes, my king. I'm on it."

He began pulling everything he had out of drawers and set it all on the table. He still had the voodoo doll in his pocket, so he got that out as well. He snarled at the object and jammed a pin in its heart, hoping the little bitch felt it. Then he opened a book that his mother had warned him about. It was a book of potent black magic that was only to be used in dire circumstances because of the risks it carried. Out of fear, he'd never even opened the book before—but he no longer had a choice. He was all in, or he'd be dead. It was time to summon the demons.

24

After a vigorous practice, Seth gathered all the Lycans and Gypsy warriors together. "The council and I haven't been able to find any other Lycans, so it looks like the thirty-five of us will have to do. Our army is strong, though, and I'm confident in our abilities. I appreciate the arduous work and dedication I've witnessed in the last few days. It will make a tremendous difference."

Gunner, who was one of the Gypsy men, raised his hand. "Excuse me, King Seth. Jile, Yanko, Stefan, and I are ready to become Lycan warriors if you'll have us. We've discussed it in great detail, and it's what we desire."

Seth looked them over and nodded. "If you want to be Lycan, I have no problem with that. I'll see to your conversions after our meeting."

"How are we going to attack them while catching them off guard?" Gerrant questioned.

Seth clasped his arms behind his back and made a path in the grass in front of them. "I'm hoping Gypsy magic will be able to see inside their camp, so we can determine how many of them there are. Then, perhaps, we can separate them with a diversion."

Caleb interjected, "What kind of diversion would be effective in capturing their interest?"

Seth looked at Marric and Mei. "Mei resembles my queen, whom they want, so if we can put a blond wig on her or lighten her hair, she can lure them to wherever it is we decide on. Would you be willing, Mei?"

She smiled and bobbed her head. "Of course. I'll do whatever I can to bring them down, and I've always wanted to go blond, so that'll be fun." She reached up and touched her light brown hair.

"Excellent. Now, some of us will have to stay here to protect the camp. Since Lycans are at home in the woods and can see in the dark, I think the Gypsy men should stay behind to guard the camp along with Jared, Yoska, and Marcus. I have no doubt some of the bloodsuckers will attack here."

"We should have the council consult the cards," Halley suggested, and he agreed.

"I'll go discuss it with them while you practice some more. Make sure to incorporate the torches, but don't light them," he commanded and headed to Ofelia's tent.

A knock on the caravan door made Julia jump up in bed. She expected it to be Elmira or Ofelia, checking up on her, but it was Sage, Wyatt's mortal wife.

"Sage, I'm surprised to see you," Julia commented with a yawn.

The woman smiled and replied, "I'm sorry. I hope I didn't wake you. I just wanted to see if you'd like to chat."

Julia arched an eyebrow and stepped aside. "Come on in. What do you want to talk about?"

Sage sat down on the small sofa. "I thought you might have questions and concerns about being married to a Lycan while you are mortal. It's out of the ordinary, so you might be doubting yourself."

Julia looked away and shrugged. "Well, I don't doubt his love or mine, but I'm worried about having children. I suppose I would be worried even if he was mortal, though, but still...Do you have kids yet?"

Sage blushed with a modest smile. "No, not yet, but we have been trying."

Julia returned the smile. "Well, that's nice, but do you worry about what it will be like for you? I have to wonder how different the pregnancy will be."

"Do you mean to ask if I think it will be like the girl from *Twilight*? No, I don't think it will be dangerous like that at all," Sage chuckled. "I think it will be like a mortal pregnancy, and the baby will be the best of us both." She rubbed her stomach and sighed.

Julia felt some relief. It was nice to have someone to talk to who knew her insecurities. "Have you thought about being turned?"

The other woman nodded. "We have discussed it and concluded that I should stay mortal."

"Oh? How come if I may ask?" Julia was intrigued.

"Well, he's mainly worried about the pain I'd experience," she admitted. "I am too."

Julia shrugged. "I haven't thought about that part. I only thought about feeling different and having to stay away from my loved ones. However, he hasn't even suggested it to me, so I suppose it doesn't really matter."

Sage patted Julia's knee. "If it matters to you, it matters. He probably hasn't suggested it because he's busy planning the battle, but he might approach you with it after the fight is over," she offered.

Julia looked down at her clasped hands. "I suppose he might. Do you ever worry that Wyatt isn't going to age, but you will until you have his child?"

"Yes, all the time. That's one of the arguments for turning me or getting pregnant as soon as possible," she replied.

"You know, if the pain is the only thing stopping you, Elmira gave an elixir to Halley to ease her suffering, and I overheard her say that it worked quite well," Julia mentioned.

"Well," Sage sighed, "I'll have to consider that; however, I need to make sure I'm not already pregnant first"—she rubbed her belly again—"and just between us, because I don't want to jinx it, I think I might be. I've been nauseous and out of sorts lately."

Julia squealed, "That's so great! For your sakes I hope you are."

"Thank you. Now, what about you? Are you going to give the king an heir sometime soon?" she wondered with a suggestive smile.

Julia blushed and shrugged. "He's brought it up, but I'm just not ready." She glanced out the window at Seth while he practiced with the others. His muscles were glistening under the bright sun. "We need to get past this battle before I can seriously consider it, and everything has happened so fast. I mean, we only knew each other for a week when I got pulled into this, and we got married."

"The prophecy, right? I heard about that," Sage responded. "It must've been overwhelming for you."

Julia fingered her wedding band. "Yes, it was. He made me fall in love, though, and being a queen is kind of cool. I just wish the future of the world didn't depend on us," she said wistfully. "It's a lot of pressure."

Sage nodded and looked out the window. "Well, I think I'm going to help the ladies with dinner. We missed lunch because—"

"Because they were rescuing me," Julia interrupted. "I feel bad about that. I can't believe I fell victim to Brad's magic."

Sage patted her arm. "It's not your fault, and they were able to save you in time."

Julia's hand flew to her neck. "Yeah, just in time…" She shuddered to think what would have happened if she'd been turned. Surely, no Lycan had been married to a vampire before.

She followed Sage outside to help with preparing dinner for the camp. Every now and then, she stole a glance at her handsome husband while he fiercely battled the other Lycans. He was strong, virile, gorgeous, sexy, heroic, and all hers. She wouldn't have it any other way.

.

Dust flew off the crinkly yellowed pages as Brad began flipping through the thick book. Drawings of demons stared at him with accusing glares as he glanced over the spells, which were written in Romani. Several incantations piqued his interest, and he dog-eared the pages to revisit them later. However, he was particularly interested in finding something to break through the Gypsies' protective magic. He needed to see inside their camp. He needed to see Julia.

He got half-way through the book when he found something that might work. He used two mirrors, black candles, and an amulet he'd once stolen from a good Gypsy. He placed the mirrors opposite each other with the two candles in between. Once the smoke from the candles swirled over both mirrors, he dangled the amulet in between them, so its image was reflected in both.

He chanted, "În această noapte şi în această oră, sparge lumina şi distruge puterea lor. Între două oglinzi, între două lumi, Arată-mi duşmanul şi destinul care se desfăşoară." *On this night and in this hour, break through the light and destroy their power. Between two mirrors, between two worlds, show me my enemy and the destiny that unfolds.*

He swung the pendent hard into one of the mirrors, cracking it, and then looked into the other to see the answers he sought. The vision made him stumble backward—it was Ofelia.

"So, the little Gypsy somehow survived her swan dive," he grumbled to himself. "No wonder magic is on their side. Well, not for long."

While he was tapped into their world, he needed to lay down a curse. He flipped back through the book until he found a juicy one, literally. It was the dead water curse. He needed water that either washed the dead or came from a cemetery, so he took a bowl to the basement and, while wearing rubber gloves to protect himself, he dipped Zephryne's hand into the bowl. She was technically dead after all.

Back upstairs, he put several droplets onto the mirror that reflected the Gypsy camp. Finally, he took his knife and nicked himself, spilling a couple drops of blood onto the mirror as well. His blood, when mixed with the dead water, would inflict his curse on the entire camp. Their water for drinking, cooking, and bathing would make them deathly ill. To make the effects even quicker, he picked up the mirror and poured the pink water on the voodoo doll of Julia.

If only I had one of the Lycan.

Brusque footsteps made his head snap up. The king was approaching, and he was giving him a deadly glare.

"I expect you have results for me," he demanded rather than questioned.

Brad forced a smile and pointed to the mirror, which still showed the Gypsy camp. "I do. I just cast a spell to taint their water supply as well as their beloved queen. They will all become deathly ill now."

Armand rubbed his chin. "I didn't tell you to kill the woman. I told you to bring her to me," he chided.

Brad still held his smile. "I can still do that in time for you to turn her before she dies. Your immortal embrace will only strengthen her."

"But not her king," Armando added. "That might work; however, be sure to get her here before it's too late."

Brad looked down at the mirror. "I'll keep watch on the camp, so I'll know when to fetch her."

"Let me know first," the king barked. "I still want the satisfaction of destroying their army. We will all go and share in the festivities."

Brad nodded in understanding. "I'm sure it will be a delightful bloodbath."

While her vindictive husband was at the house working Brad over, Melanie followed Craig on his hunt in the woods to work him over.

The man spun around when he heard twigs snapping behind him. "Oh, it's you. I was worried it was one of those blasted beasts," he sighed in relief.

She swayed her hips seductively while making her approach. "You'd be able to smell those stinky bastards. They smell like musty wet dogs," she chuckled softly.

He returned her smile, but his eyes darted everywhere. "Is the king with you, or are you hunting by yourself?"

She nestled up to him and ran her long fingernail down the front of his shirt. "Actually, I'm hunting *you*. I've been hoping to get you alone ever since the day you joined us."

His brows furrowed. "Oh yeah? Is that because I tasted good?"

Melanie leaned in and traced his bottom lip with the tip of her tongue. "You tasted delicious, but that's not what I'm after."

Craig grabbed her wrist and spun her around, pinning her against a massive oak tree. "Is this what you want? Do you want to be manhandled by me?" he hissed with a sensuous grin.

"It's exactly what I want," she responded and cupped his erection, straining against his jeans.

He pulled on her wrist to take her deeper into the woods, so they were farther away from Brad's domain and the vampire king. Then they tore away each other's clothes and shared a frenzied encounter filled with pure lust.

Elmira rushed through the camp to Ofelia's tent. "I was looking at the cards when an uneasy feeling came over me, so I tapped into our line's magic. We've been found, and a curse was placed upon this camp," she exclaimed with her words rushed together.

Ofelia shot up from the ground. "Oh no! We'll have to quickly leave these grounds," she yelped and ran out of the tent to holler at their people and the Lycans. After everyone was gathered, she explained, "A curse has been placed on this camp, so we must leave immediately for a new location. Pack up and prepare to leave within the hour."

"Where can we go?" Jeric, one of the Gypsy men, inquired. The others looked at her for her response too. They all shared the same concern.

Caleb stood up and responded before Ofelia had the chance to answer. "We can go back to our land in Modesto. We have plenty of acres to camp on," he offered.

"No. That will spread us out too much when it's time for the battle. We'll be split too far apart from the camp. I say we stay nearby," Seth interjected.

Elmira cleared her throat loud enough to capture his attention. "I have clients who have a large piece of land at Echo Park Lake, which isn't that far from here, and they've invited us to camp there whenever we want to. I can call them to make sure the offer still stands." She pulled her phone out without even waiting for him to approve.

Excited chatter broke out between the Gypsies and the Lycans while they waited for their future to be laid out. Elmira quickly hung up and waved to the crowd to get its attention.

"They said we are invited to stay on their land for as long as we desire," she announced. "Of course, that means I owe them free readings for life now, but no worries," she added with a little smirk.

"All right then. Let's get packed up and get out of here," Ofelia commanded, and the group sprang into action.

Before they left their location, the council got together and cast a cloaking spell to block the black magic interfering in their lives because they didn't want the enemy to see their new camp site. They also cast a curse reversal spell to reflect the curse back to the one who cast it, and they made sure that every member in the camp wore a protection amulet or talisman to ward off future attempts. It was their strongest gathering of magic since they'd caused the earthquake to free the Lycan king from his tomb.

A little over an hour later, they were settled at their new location. Luckily for them, they used cars to move their wagons instead of horses, so the trip didn't take as long, and it wasn't as arduous as it would've been when traveling on the highways.

The home owners made sure that they were comfortable and helped them tap into the water supply. Of course, they were oblivious to the Lycans and the battle that was looming ahead.

"How are you going to practice now?" Julia asked Seth while scratching Oscar's belly. She wasn't feeling well, so she went back to bed after helping the others set up as much as she could.

"Well, we can go into the forest if we need to, but I think we've practiced enough. I'm confident in their abilities," he answered while looking out the window. "I just hope the vampires don't attack us here. We can't risk the exposure to humans. They'd never understand that we are protecting them."

She climbed out of bed to comfort him, but suddenly became dizzy and fell back onto it. "Whoa," she exclaimed while he rushed to her side. "The room is spinning."

"Lie back down, and I'll go see if Elmira can help. Maybe she has medicine you can have," he offered and quickly departed.

Oscar stayed with her and nuzzled himself close with a whimper. "I know, buddy. I'll be all right, though," she soothed her friend. "I'm already feeling better."

Seth returned a few minutes later with a mug of hot tea. "This is a recipe that should help," he said and handed it to her. "Be careful; it's hot."

Julia took a tentative sip. "It's different, but it's not bad. It tastes like flowers, but not chamomile."

He shrugged. "She didn't say what's in it, but I'm sure it's good for you, and hopefully, it will help. I can't have my queen feeling sick." He climbed in next to her and wrapped his arm protectively around her shoulders.

"I'm already feeling better. I think it was just the excitement of the day getting to me," she conjectured. "I'm glad Elmira figured things out before it was too late."

"Me—"

A loud shout outside broke him off, and he leapt from the bed and ran to the door. He saw several people running toward Ofelia's tent.

"Something's up. I'll go check it out," he tossed over his shoulder and bolted down the steps.

Curious, Julia climbed out of bed and followed behind him. Just as she reached Ofelia's tent, Seth emerged with a sad face.

"She's gone," he told the onlookers before noticing her standing there. "Darling, you should be resting," he mumbled as he approached her.

"Who's gone? What's going on?" Julia questioned him, ignoring his concern for her.

He glanced over his shoulder at the weeping women and men. "The young Gypsy woman, Netta, has died. She became suddenly ill, and there was nothing they could do for her."

Julia clutched her stomach as it began to roil. "From what?" She pleaded with her eyes for him not to tell her that it had to do with the curse.

He shook his head. "I'm not sure. I'm waiting for Ofelia or Elmira to tell me."

Just then, Elmira stepped out of the tent and announced, "It was the curse that took our poor darling Netta. Ofelia looked through the magic portal and saw water, which means the dead water curse must've been used. That is serious black magic, and we'll be lucky if no one else falls victim. So, if you have any water from the former site stored, dump it. Then destroy the containers."

Seth stared in shock at Julia, and he waved Elmira over to them.

"What is it, Seth?" she wondered.

He looked from Julia to her and then back to Julia's pale face. "What about Julia? Since she was feeling ill, I'm worried," he voiced.

Elmira put the back of her hand to Julia's forehead and then her cheeks. "She's a little clammy, but she doesn't feel feverish. Tell me, Julia, did you drink the water before we left the camp?"

Julia shook her head. "No, but I had some milk. Do I have to worry about that?"

The older woman clasped her hand in hers. "No, it was just the water supply that had been cursed, and the water I used for your tea came from these grounds. You were probably just exhausted, or perhaps it has to do with the vampire's bite, but don't worry. You have a powerful amulet, and it will offer you valuable protection. Even if something made you ill, you shouldn't share Netta's fate."

Julia cringed as two men brought the lifeless body out on a stretcher. "What happens now?"

Elmira followed her stare. "We'll have to burn her body to kill the infection. If we bury her, it will affect the soil and make others succumb to it," she answered grimly.

"We're sorry for your loss," Julia whispered hoarsely and clasped her husband's hand. It felt reassuring to have him close by.

Elmira nodded and then walked away to comfort the girl's family members.

27

ℬrad was beside himself with worry. He'd gone into the kitchen to fix a bite to eat, and when he got back to the mirrors, the vision of the Gypsy camp was gone. For the second time, he cast the spell to let him look inside their camp, but it didn't work.

He paced the carpet around the table, rubbing his clammy palms together. "He's going to kill me," he stated to himself with a high-pitched laugh. "Yep, he's going to rip my head off with his teeth."

Luckily for him, the vampire king had gone out hunting again. It gave him time to figure something out. He flipped through the book of black magic, searching for plan B, when he found something that was risky but possibly helpful. He found a spell for haunting.

He pulled his Ouija board out of the drawer and began chanting the spell from the book. He was attempting to contact Tressa's spirit. He would've used someone from his family line, but the spell was more potent with a fresh spirit—someone who didn't have a firm hold on the ghostly plane yet.

"Tressa, I seek your help and guidance. Come forth before me," he spoke aloud. Nothing happened, so he tried again. "Tressa, I seek your assistance. Show yourself to me."

A cold draft blew through the room, extinguishing the black candle, and he knew he'd successfully contacted her—or someone. While he stared in awe, an apparition appeared and floated over the table. It was Tressa, and she wasn't happy to be there.

"Why did you summon me?" she barked. "What do you want?"

Brad's throat suddenly felt dry, and he had to swallow hard to find his voice. "I need your guidance. I seek your help." His voice came out high-pitched, and sweat rolled down his forehead to burn his eyes.

"And why would I help you? You didn't help me," she seethed.

He shifted his weight from one foot to the other and back again. "I had no idea that Armando was going to kill you. Be mad at him, not me. The Gypsy girl, Ofelia, survived your push off the bluffs, and she is helping the Lycans with their army. I need your help to curse the camp. They thwarted my prior attempt."

She broke out in raucous laughter and clasped her transparent hands together. "And why should I care? I'm dead after all."

Brad looked into her glowing eyes. "What if helping me could bring you back? Would you be interested then?" he fished.

"I'm listening," she stated and crossed her arms.

"You can keep the body you possess. I know a spell to make it so," he answered.

"Hmm…Then I could get my revenge on the king," she suggested with a malicious grin. "But who do you intend for me to possess? It would have to be someone worth my while."

Brad rubbed his clammy hands together to warm them up. "How about the Lycan queen? Would that be worth your while? She's in the same camp as Ofelia."

"Perhaps. That would give me access to the Gypsy, and since they are going after Armando, it would help me with that revenge too." She cackled loudly, and he hoped no one else in the house heard her.

"Do we have a deal then?" he questioned. He needed to wrap things up before the king returned because he would certainly not approve.

"Yes, work your black magic and bring me back," she demanded.

Armando stalked the forest, looking for his queen. He'd told her they'd hunt together, so he was suspicious of her going alone. It didn't take him long to sniff her out, and he found her having sex with Craig. His blood boiled as he approached the clueless couple.

"What do you think you're doing?" he demanded in a fierce, guttural growl.

The two lovers scrambled backward, tugging on their clothes to put them back in place.

"K-k-king Ar-Ar-Armando," Craig stuttered while fumbling with his pants button. "She followed me into the forest and seduced me, Sire."

Melanie glared at the stammering idiot. "I did not!" she screeched. "You came onto me."

"Enough!" Armando bellowed, and birds scattered from the treetops. "You're lying to me," he accused and looked from one adulterer to the other. "And this will never happen again!"

"No, of course not," Melanie cried and stuck out her bottom lip. "I'm so sorry, my king."

Armando glared at his wife and approached her lover. He grabbed the man's head and twisted hard until his neck snapped like a twig. Then he kept twisting until it detached from the body altogether. He threw it at his cheating bride, and she screamed in fear for her own neck.

"Get up," he snarled, and she obliged with wobbly legs. "Your punishment is next."

April 18, 2014

Julia woke up nauseous and bolted out of the caravan for the utility block to dry heave. "What on earth is wrong with me?" she wondered aloud in between spasms. Elmira was coming out of the shower and stopped to check on her.

"Aren't you feeling any better today?" she asked with grave concern.

"Not yet," Julia mumbled and wiped her mouth off with some tissue.

"Let me bring you some more tea. I'll make it stronger to calm your stomach," the older woman offered. She started to walk out the door, but then she turned and asked, "Could you be with child?"

Julia froze with her eyes wide open. "No, I shouldn't be. I'm on the pill yet."

"Hmm…I'm also going to bring you another protection talisman. Just in case…" she softly stated before walking outside.

Julia's hand went to the two amulets she was already wearing. "How much more protection do I need?" she wondered. She felt scared; she was worried the curse that had killed Netta had affected her too.

Seth was pacing the ground outside the utility block when she emerged. He put one hand on her shoulder and squeezed. "What's wrong? Are you still sick?" he inquired with a furrowed brow, and his voice trembled.

She couldn't lie because he'd likely heard her retching, so she replied, "Yeah, but Elmira is getting me something for it. I think I just caught a bug."

He scooped her up into his thick arms and carried her back to the caravan. "I'm worried it could be more than that, so I want to talk to her about it. I need to know this isn't the same thing that killed Netta."

She clucked her tongue and murmured, "I've considered that too, but she died right away, and I'm just a little nauseous."

He set her down on their bed. "Well, I still want to ask her about it. She has to have a way to find out for sure."

There was a knock on their door, and Elmira called out to them. He opened the door and got right to it.

"We were just discussing you. We want to know if this could be from the curse that killed Netta," he stated dryly. "Honestly, what do you think?"

Elmira wrung her hands and looked from him to Julia and then back to him. "I don't know for absolute certain, but I don't think so. She said she didn't drink the water, and she was wearing her amulets, so the dead water curse shouldn't have an effect on her. Of course, he could've cast another one I suppose, but still, it would have a limited effect because of the necklaces." She walked over to Julia and pressed a large talisman into her palm. "Here's a powerful family heirloom that will add even more protection. Please wear all three amulets for the maximum effect."

Julia looked at the shiny piece and gasped. "I don't want to take something that is part of your heritage. I'll use something else." She tried to hand it back, but Elmira refused it.

"I insist you wear it, my queen. You can give it back after the battle," she remarked.

"Please accept it, my love," Seth chimed in. "I agree with her. Dangerous days lie ahead of us, and I need you to be as safe as possible."

Julia shrugged and pulled the necklace over her head. "If you both insist, but I am giving it back when this is over."

Elmira fingered a strand of Julia's long blond hair. "Mei is dying her hair blond this morning. I think you should color yours darker to help with the charade," she advised. "We could dye it brown, red, or black for you."

Julia fingered her mane. "Gee, I don't know. I've never colored my hair before."

"It's for your safety, sweetheart," Seth advised. Then, with a wink, he added, "And I wouldn't mind seeing you as a redhead."

She raised a brow at him but relented. "All right, you heard the boss. Red it is."

Elmira clapped her hands together like a happy child. "Excellent. Come with me to my tent and we'll fix you up. You won't recognize yourself when we're done."

"I bet you'll be very sexy," Seth encouraged her. "I can't wait to see it"—he glanced out the window—"I'm going to take the Lycans into the woods for some field practice and to hunt. Don't worry, though, because we won't go far, and we'll stay out of sight."

She gave him a little wave as she stepped outside. "Have fun."

Seth and the others sniffed the air for vampire stench after they shifted into their monstrous selves. The air was clean, so they relaxed and hunted for food, and after eating, they engaged in mock combat.

He addressed the group after they shifted back. "I think we're ready to attack. The Gypsy warriors are strong and fierce like us, and there's no sense in putting it off any longer. We can always attack in waves if we need to, but after the curse they laid down on us, I just don't think we can wait."

Marric was the first to respond. "You are our king, and we will do as you say. Will we attack today then?"

Everyone looked eagerly at him, anticipating his response. "Yes, we'll start today. Mei is transforming into a blond, and the queen is changing her look too, so we'll use Mei as bait while we hang back, and then we'll attack, taking them by surprise."

"So, we'll be going toward their hideaway then because as far as we know, they don't know where we are, right?" Logan asked.

Seth nodded in affirmation. "That's correct. I'm certain they are holed up at the dark Gypsy's home in the forest. I have no way to know how many vampires they've turned, but I'm certain we'll do surmountable damage. Then, if need be, we can always try to find more soldiers." He crossed the grass in front of them with confident strides. "On the other hand, though, the queen has been feeling ill, so I want to be sure she's okay before we go. If she's still sick today, we'll wait until tomorrow. I can't leave her when she's vulnerable."

They all nodded and murmured in agreement before breaking up and heading back to camp. Seth couldn't wait to see his redheaded beauty.

Melanie pulled against her shackles until they cut into her flesh. In his fit of rage, Armando had chained her to the wall in the basement. In addition to the discomfort it caused, it was humiliating since the others were gawking at her.

"Stop staring at me," she hissed at the onlookers, "or I'll rip your eyes out when I'm freed."

They turned away, but she heard them whispering about her, and it made her fume. She supposed the punishment was better than what Armando had inflicted on Craig, but still, it wasn't befitting a queen.

"Zephryne," Armando suddenly called out from the top of the stairs, and the vampire slunk her way up them. Soon, she returned with a bag of blood and approached Melanie.

"Have some breakfast. You need to keep your strength up," Zephryne told her.

Melanie choked out, "My strength for battle?"

Zephryne smiled sadistically. "That or phase two of your punishment."

"Oh," she replied and took a healthy sip.

Armando had been correct about the preserved blood not tasting good like the real thing, but she would cope. She tried to take another swallow, but Zephryne pulled it away.

"The king said only one sip," she said cattily and gave the remaining fluid to the newborns. Then she retreated upstairs.

It wasn't too much longer when Melanie heard Armando's heavy footsteps headed toward the door, and her dead heart lurched in her chest. *What's phase two of my punishment?* The parts of her body that could move trembled violently, making the chains clatter, and she tried to swallow, but her dry mouth and throat made it impossible.

The door swung open, and he came down the stairs, heading straight toward her with a glare in his beady red eyes. She could see saliva dripping from his fangs, and it made her stomach churn. She was afraid to speak, so she kept her lips tightly closed.

"Are you hungry this morning, my dear?" he asked, finally breaking the silence. "Would you like to hunt?"

She tried to maintain eye contact, but he looked so angry. She averted his piercing stare and softly answered, "Yes, I'm famished. Can I hunt with you or for you? I could bring you back a tasty morsel."

"No," he answered sharply. "You haven't learned your lesson yet."

She looked up with teary eyes. "Oh, but I have. I'm so sorry about my betrayal, and I'd like to make it up to you."

His glare intensified, and he turned on his heel to storm away from her.

"Please don't leave me like this," she pleaded, but it fell on deaf ears.

He nodded to the newborns, and they followed him up the stairs. She was left alone and helpless.

Brad waited for the vampires to go hunting before he summoned Tressa's spirit again. He knew his cousin was chained up in the basement, but there was nothing he could do for her, and he needed to work his magic with Tressa before the others returned.

Tressa appeared on the first try, and she smiled vindictively at him. "I'm ready to do this," she exclaimed. "I'm ready to feel life again."

Brad worried. "This might not be that easy," he advised. "She's heavily protected by charms."

Tressa pointed a transparent finger at him. "Do not fail me," she threatened.

"I'm certainly not going to try to," he replied. "However, they have a lot of good magic on their side."

She crossed her arms. "Well, we'll just see what happens then. There has to be a way in somehow," she speculated.

He used the mirror spell first, but it still wasn't working. Next, he used the voodoo doll and Julia's photograph, but he still felt his magic being blocked.

"I have an idea that might work," Tressa announced with frustration in her voice. "I'll go to her and overtake her body that way."

Brad bit his bottom lip and considered her plan. "I feel, though, that her talismans will still block you."

She smiled cattily. "That's why you'll have to go with me to remove them from her pretty little neck."

"That won't be easy. She is wary of me," he warned.

Tressa still wore her cocky smile. "That's why I'm going to teach you how to glamour. I'll make you look like someone she trusts, so you can get close to her."

"Ofelia," he blurted out. "She trusts the Gypsy. Of course, her husband would be another option to consider."

Tressa shook her head. "Since I know what the Gypsy looks like, we'll use her. We need three red candles, rose oil, a quartz crystal, and a mirror."

Brad scurried around the room gathering the needed items. After he lit the candles, he looked up to her for her next instruction.

"Close your eyes and focus on her face. Tell me when you can see her clearly."

He took a deep breath and concentrated on the Gypsy girl. "Okay, I can."

"I can see her too, so let's begin."

She chanted her spell and told him to open his eyes, drip wax from each candle onto the mirror, add three drops of rose oil to the wax, and then dip the quartz in it until it was coated.

"Now, look at your reflection," she told him, and he obeyed.

Brad gasped and leapt backward. "I look like her," he exclaimed and touched his face. His fingers felt stubble, though, so he was confused. He touched his hair, and it felt the same as usual, but it was long in the reflection. He looked up at Tressa for an explanation. "Did I change? Do you see her when you look at me?"

The ghostly witch laughed. "Yes, I can see her and so will everyone else, including you. However, you didn't actually change your appearance. It's just a temporary illusion. With that said, we need to hurry and go to her."

"Okay, but how do I take you along for the ride?" he questioned.

"I will possess the voodoo doll, and then you'll release me when we get there," she answered. "Just say the phrase *I release you* three times while holding the object."

Brad heard voices outside. "Okay, do it now. Armando's back."

Julia gawked into the handheld mirror, and her hand ran through her red tresses. She couldn't get over the difference the color made.

"Different isn't it?" Mei asked as she touched her own changed hair.

Julia nodded. "It sure is. I hope Seth likes it because I'm tempted to keep it for a while."

Elmira patted her on the back, and her reflection beamed at her in the mirror. "You look stunning, and it's going to knock his socks off."

Julia stood up as she heard the men returning to the camp. "I suppose it's time to find out."

When she stepped out of Ofelia's tent, she saw Seth heading for their caravan. With a smile playing on her lips, she snuck up behind him and tapped his shoulder. He spun around in surprise, and his mouth turned up in a wide grin.

"You are absolutely gorgeous, my queen," he raved. "I love your new hairdo. I think it's extremely sexy."

She winked at him. "Oh yeah? Does that mean you're in the mood?" she flirted.

"I'm always in the mood for you, but are you sure you're feeling better?" he questioned with concern. "I don't want you overdoing it."

In truth, she did feel better. "Yes, I'm feeling fine," she assured him. "Let me show you"—she pointed to her hair—"Red on the head means a fire in the bed."

Seth laughed at her boisterous flirting. He wanted to take her to the heights of passion, but he needed to plan the first attack. However, when going into battle, there was always a risk, so he gave in to their lusty desires. He swept her up in his arms and carried her the rest of the way to their caravan.

He took his time loving and worshipping her body, kissing every inch of flesh. "You're so sexy," he growled. "I can't believe my luck to have you as my queen."

"Forever and ever," she declared with a satisfied smile before encouraging him to lie on his back, so she could kiss her way down his body and then take him inside her mouth.

"Oh God, woman, you're killing me," he groaned as she teased him with her tongue.

She climbed up his body and impaled herself with his iron-hard tumescence. She took her time sliding down his length while she watched pleasure contort his face. When his aching need filled her, she rocked her body back and forth, grinding her hips into his while her hands ran up his hard ripple of muscles. Then she leaned forward to take his right bud into her mouth while bouncing her hips up and down, completely coating him with her arousal. She moved her mouth to his and nibbled on his bottom lip before darting her tongue inside the welcoming heat.

Seth wrapped his arms tightly around his redheaded vixen and rolled her onto her back to drive himself inside her and take control of the lovemaking. He flexed his hips over and over, giving her everything he had.

Julia answered his thrusting hips by arching hers into them to meet each possessive lunge. They collided in perfect rhythm for several minutes before a mutual finale exploded behind their eyes. When he rolled off to her side, she nestled herself underneath his arm, sprawling across his chest.

"I love you," she whispered while her breathing returned to normal.

He squeezed her reassuringly. "And I love you, my goddess."

"Can we stay like this forever?" she sighed.

Seth kissed the top of her head and ran his fingers down her side. "I wish we could, my love. I need to get up, though, because we are attacking the enemy today. I can't let them figure out our hoax and come after you again. I also have to protect everyone in this camp."

"And all of mankind," she added with a grimace. "I knew this moment was coming, but I don't think I'm emotionally prepared for it."

He squeezed her again before climbing out of bed. "Don't worry, my love. I promise I'll be coming back to you. You just be sure to keep yourself safe. I'll be leaving the Gypsy men and a few of the Lycans here for protection, but you should be prepared for anything. Remember that you can only kill a vampire by decapitation or fire."

She made a sour face. "Hopefully, they won't come here, but I won't forget."

They both left the caravan to gather the others. Once everyone was seated, Seth explained that it was time to make their move on the vampires.

"Mei will go into the woods, wearing Julia's clothes, so they can pick up her scent. We'll be waiting in the wings for our attack. After we take out the first group, we can go to the dark Gypsy's lair to find and destroy the rest of them," he explained.

Elmira raised her hand to interrupt. "I have an idea that should help you. Vampires can smell you just like you can them, right?" Seth nodded, so she continued with her idea. "We can rub you down with an ointment to mask your scent. That way you'll for sure have the element of surprise."

Seth clapped his hands together. "That's an excellent idea. Get the supplies necessary while we change."

Seth explained the plan of attack to the others, and then they changed. By the time they finished, Elmira had the herbal ointment ready, and they slathered it on to mask their scent. Then Jared, Yoska, and Marcus took their posts within the camp along with the Gypsy men, who were heavily armed. The women, including Julia, built a large bonfire and had torches ready to light if they needed them. Then they bid the Lycans good-bye and good luck as they followed Mei into the woods with Seth in the lead.

"I just hope the homeowners don't come down here," Elmira worried aloud. "They shouldn't be able to see us because of the trees, but they might hear the fighting if it comes to that."

Julia patted her arm and replied, "Well, we can't exactly tell them what to expect, so there's nothing we can do about that now." A tear trickled down her cheek as her husband and the others disappeared from sight.

"My queen, I know you're worried, and that's understandable, but our king knows what he's doing. This is his prophecy after all—his destiny to fulfill," Elmira assured her.

Julia tried to smile at the concerned woman. "I know it is, but that doesn't make it easier. Shall I help you with lunch?" She needed something to distract her.

"Certainly," Elmira chirped, and they joined the other women in the meal preparation.

Brad couldn't risk crossing paths with the vampires since he would look like Ofelia to them, so he snuck out the back door and around the house once they were all inside. Then he slunk into the woods and began to run. Once he was a safe distance away, he slowed down to catch his breath, and he chanted the magic words to set Tressa free from the voodoo doll.

He didn't know where the new Gypsy camp was, but if he went to the old one, he could tap into his powers to hopefully find it by using the crystals he'd brought with him.

He never expected to come across Julia in the woods, so he couldn't believe his luck when he did.

"Julia," he called out in surprise, "what are you doing here? I don't think it's safe for you to be out here."

When he drew closer, Brad realized the blond wasn't the Lycan queen. "Oh, I'm sorry. I thought you were my friend. You look like her from a distance."

Mei stared at the fake Ofelia. She and everyone else at the camp had seen Julia with her red hair, not to mention Ofelia had stayed there to guard it, so she instantly knew that dark magic was at play. She quickly shrugged off Julia's dress, shifted, and swiped her large hand at the imposter before he had time to run away. Huge gashes splayed across the fraud's chest, breaking his black magic and revealing a man she'd never seen before. The fatally wounded man stumbled backward, trying to stop the rush of blood spilling out of his body. His eyes bulged and darted around, searching for an escape route, but by that point, several other Lycans had him surrounded, including the Lycan king.

Seth couldn't believe his luck. Without any hesitation, he pounced on Brad and ripped into his throat with his blood-thirsty fangs while his claws tore into the screaming man's legs. Soon, Brad's cries became nothing more than a gurgle, and his body was nothing more than ripped flesh and blood. Seth stood back, admiring his handiwork with smug satisfaction. He conveyed his thoughts to the others.

Excellent job, Mei. He is the dark Gypsy who cursed the camp.

She responded with her thoughts. *He looked like Ofelia, but I knew it wasn't her.*

Everyone, be alert for other traps. We have no way to know what other magic he performed before his demise. If the vampires aren't in the woods, then they must be at his house.

Mei asked him, *Do you want me to shift back into human form in case we cross others?*

No, Brad and Melanie are the only ones who know what she looks like, and Melanie would probably see through the ruse right away. Let's proceed as we are.

Tressa's spirit was still floating in the trees, and she was wondering what to do. Brad was just a puppet, so she didn't really need him to carry out her plans. She could still possess the Lycan queen and seek her revenge against Armando, or she could possess Ofelia to have access to power. That made the most sense.

She possessed a hawk's body and flew over the city until she found the Gypsy camp. Then she landed in a nearby tree and scanned the camp for her victim. She found her wandering the grounds, and the bird's heart raced. She sat still, watching the Gypsy leader for a few minutes before exiting the bird's body and floating toward her.

Armando paced the house with angry steps. He didn't know where Brad was, but he assumed the Gypsy wasn't out fetching the Lycan queen for him. He was likely avoiding him because he'd failed yet again. In his fit of rage, Armando ordered Zephryne to go find the Gypsy and drag him back to the house. He was out of patience with the man. It was time to show Brad what happened when he pissed off the vampire king.

The front door swung open, and Zephryne entered alone. "Well? Where is he?" Armando demanded.

Zephryne held up Brad's Black Dragon amulet. "I'm sorry, my king, but this is all that is left of him. I found his remains in the forest. It looks like a wild animal got to him."

Armando raised an eyebrow. "A wild animal or a Lycan?"

"I didn't smell Lycan on him, my king," she quickly responded.

He opened his hands with a shrug. "Well, no big deal. I was done with him anyway. Now go gather the others. I'm ready to find that damn Gypsy camp," he commanded.

She bowed her head and excused herself to the basement. While she was gone, he browsed Brad's black magic books, and an idea came to him. Maybe his bride had some usefulness left in her. He went down the stairs as the others filed up them.

"I'll be right there," he mentioned to Zephryne. "I need to speak to Melanie."

Melanie tensed at the mention of her name. *Is he going to inflict more punishment on me?* She silently prayed for redemption as he approached her.

Armando stopped directly in front of her and stared hard into her frightened eyes. "Sorry to inform you, *dear wife*, but your cousin is dead. Before you ask, no, I didn't kill him; although, I was about to. It appears, however, that he crossed a bear or something in the woods."

Melanie felt stunned. She didn't really care for Brad, but his demise meant that he wouldn't be around to help her, not that he'd offered.

"Anyway," Armando continued, "this might bode well for you. Since you are his relation, you should be able to tap into the black magic he was using and finish the tasks at hand. I want the Lycan queen brought to me on her knees. Do you think you can accomplish that?"

Melanie swallowed hard, and it burned her parched throat. "I will do my best not to fail you," she whispered hoarsely. "I'll drag her here by her hair if I have to."

He wrapped his clawed hand tightly around her neck. "You'd better not fail me, or you'll share your cousin's fate," he hissed.

When he let go of her, she replied, "I understand," and a tear ran down her cheek. Her life was at risk no matter what. Either he'd kill her or the Lycans would, unless, by some miracle, she was successful.

Armando undid her chains and led her up the stairs since she was weak. Then he got her a bag of blood from the refrigerator.

"Drink this. It's not as good as fresh blood, but it will give you some of your strength back until you can hunt for prey," he ordered, and she complied without question.

While it wasn't as good, it did quench her thirst, and she immediately started to feel better. She felt well enough, in fact, to return the evil glare Zephryne was giving her. The vampire obviously had a problem with her.

"Go to the book that Brad was looking at and find a spell to locate the Gypsy camp," Armando ordered her and handed over the Black Dragon amulet, which she quickly donned. Then he cleared his throat to get everyone's attention. "I've gathered you all because the time has come for us to begin the battle. We will scour the woods for Lycans, while my queen finds the Gypsy camp and brings the Lycan slut to me. Our diversion in the woods will make it easier for her. Kill every Lycan you see in the manner you've been taught. Remember, you must decapitate them. Luckily, in addition to your claws and fangs, our host has an impressive collection of swords and knives. Take what you need, and let's get on with it."

He gestured to the room that housed the artillery, and the blood-thirsty vampires wasted no time in helping themselves to the assortment of weaponry while Melanie continued flipping through the book of black magic.

Once they were armed, they followed their king outside to begin the hunt. Melanie quickly ran in a different direction but not before Armando pulled her aside.

"Don't think that I won't find you if you run off. It would be a fate worse than death for you," he hissed in her ear.

"I have no intentions of displeasing you further," she replied with her chin held high. "I'll bring her back here and chain her to the wall for you."

He licked his fangs. "See that you do. She'll make an excellent meal for me." He flicked his hand to wave her away, and she took off running.

Melanie ran to Chinatown to pick up the Gypsies' scent trail. She used the spell Brad had been reading in the book of black magic along with a map and a crystal to scry for the new camp. It didn't take her long to get the crystal to drop on the map.

"So, you're hiding at Echo Park Lake. I know where that is," she said aloud with a smile. "Ready or not, here I come."

She boarded a trolley, fighting her thirst for blood, and was near the park in no time at all. A man, who'd been eyeing her appreciatively during the ride, made the grave error of following her off.

"Hey, pretty lady, where are you running off to in such a hurry?" the Latino hollered at her.

Once the trolley was out of sight, she spun around and attacked. She quickly drained him and left his carcass by the road.

"Let the police try to figure that out," she mused aloud and went on her way toward the camp, feeling stronger than ever.

33

The powerful amulets Ofelia wore foiled Tressa's plans. Disheartened, she floated above the camp while thinking of a new strategy. She decided to find another body to possess—a Gypsy with less protection. That way, she could attack Ofelia, remove the amulets, and then possess her. However, when her sights landed squarely on a young woman who wasn't wearing a necklace, someone else caught her eye. Melanie was lurking in the trees, and Ofelia could see the saliva dripping from her vampire fangs.

So, you're a vampire now. That's even better! With your vampire strength and Gypsy magic, I'll be unstoppable.

When she got close to her, being sure to stay out of everyone's sight, she noticed the Black Dragon amulet hanging between the vampire's breasts. Since she'd weakened Brad's amulet when she was alive, it wouldn't pose an issue for her. With the right words, she entered the vampire's body and read her thoughts. Melanie was there for Julia, which was fine, but Tressa wanted Ofelia first.

She shared her own ambitions with the vampire. *I need your body to get to the Gypsy leader, Ofelia. Then I'll help you get the Lycan queen. You can try to fight me, but it won't do you any good.*

Melanie quietly agreed to comply with the ghostly witch. She hadn't spotted Julia among the crowd yet anyway.

She watched Ofelia as the woman patrolled the camp and waited until she was alone to pounce on her. To her surprise, the Gypsy was stronger than she looked, but Melanie used her dagger to cut away the amulets, and then she bolted for the cover of the trees.

Ofelia was completely caught off guard, but she quickly recovered. She opened her mouth to scream, but then something overcame her. Something forced her to keep quiet about the attack. She got back up and continued to walk the perimeter as if nothing happened.

Meanwhile, Melanie hid in the treetops, looking for any sign of alert. Apparently, the witch had been honest about letting her get to Julia, so she descended the tree and circled back around the camp. Finally, she found her. Julia had dyed her hair red, but that didn't hide her from her former best friend. Melanie ate the queen up with hungry eyes as she entered a caravan all by herself.

When no one was looking, she ran up the steps and opened the door. Unfortunately for her, Julia's dog was inside, and he lunged with a fierce growl, tackling her back down the stairs while Julia let out a blood-curdling scream.

Oscar had a good grip on Melanie's throat, but she was stronger and tossed him off before running as fast as she could for the trees. The entire camp was alerted and after her, so she had to find a hiding spot.

Julia sat on the ground, holding her growling dog in a tight hug while she wept. "Thank God you were here for me, Ossie," she cried and stroked his fur.

The three Lycan men ran up to her first. "We didn't smell the vampire until it was too late, my queen. We were following its trail when you screamed," Yoska explained. "I'm so sorry we failed to protect you and the camp."

Julia looked up at the new Lycan and forced herself to smile. "It's all right, Yoska. This is all new for you. I know you mean to keep us all safe."

He turned to Ofelia as she approached. "Shall the three of us go after her?" he asked, gesturing to Marcus and Jared.

She surprised them, though, when she replied, "No. We'll all go. Where there's one vampire, there are more. Let's flush them out now."

Elmira interrupted, "But what about the camp? Surely, you want some of the men to stay behind for our sakes."

Ofelia looked at her and scowled. "No. We'll all go after the vampires as I've said. You'll be fine here. They won't come back now that the camp is on alert."

Elmira looked at the younger woman with a wary eye. "What do you think, my queen?" she asked Julia.

Julia looked at her with a blank stare and then at Ofelia. "I'm not good at these things, so I guess do what she says. I don't feel I'm qualified to be in charge for something like this."

As the Gypsy warriors, including Ofelia, and Lycans filed toward the woods, the women in the camp lit torches, and Elmira stood protectively by Julia.

"Something is wrong," the Gypsy whispered to her. "Ofelia wasn't wearing her amulets, and she would never leave her people unprotected like this."

Julia accepted a lit torch. "Then I have to do something about it. I have to go after them," she replied.

Elmira's eyes opened wide. "You can't do that. That would be too dangerous for you, my queen."

Julia sighed, "Exactly, I'm the queen, and that makes this my responsibility. My people are out there, including my husband. If something is amiss with Ofelia, I need to warn them. Keep Oscar here with you. He'll alert you if any other vampires are nearby."

"No, I'm going with you," Elmira barked, her tone taking Julia by surprise. "If Ofelia has been possessed, as I assume she has, you'll need me. I can rid her of the spirit. I just need to grab something from my caravan."

Julia sighed and looked around at the others. "I suppose I will need you then. We need to do everything we can to save her too."

They took off running, only stopping long enough to grab a potion from Elmira's caravan and to leave Oscar with Inga, one of the Gypsy women. It was obvious he wanted to go with Julia, but she wouldn't put him at risk.

"Watch him," she told Inga. "He'll alert you if a vampire is nearby." The woman nodded as the Lycan queen and Gypsy matriarch took off for the woods.

Neither woman spotted Melanie, who had just fed on a fisherman at the lake to regain her strength. The dog's vicious bite had hurt her worse than she'd originally thought. He wasn't her concern at the moment, though. His *mommy* was. She followed the women into the thick forest.

Seth led the other Lycans through the thick underbrush toward Brad's dwelling. They carefully sniffed the air for vampire stench, happy that Elmira's ointment still kept the Lycan scent masked.

Gerrant was close to Seth, and he came to a sudden halt. *I think I saw something over to the far left.*

Seth looked south, where his soldier indicated, but he didn't see anything, and he couldn't smell anything either, not even evidence of animal life. *I don't see anything, but let's fan out a little wider just to cover our bases. If we can mask our scent, it's possible they did too.*

They continued pressing forward toward the cabin when a loud yelp pierced the air as two vampires ran toward them with swords raised above their heads. Seth ducked the swipe of the blade as a small female vampire lunged at him. He quickly came up with his arm extended, lashing his claws across her abdomen. The force lifted her off the ground, and when she came back down, his follow-up blow caught her neck and severed her head with ease.

Gerrant and Aric both took on the other vampire, who was larger and more experienced than the female. He sliced his weapon through the air, catching Aric's shoulder. Before he could swing again, though, Gerrant tackled him to the ground and chomped his neck until the head detached. The crunching of bones and ripping of flesh filled the air along with the strong metallic odor of blood.

Seth checked on Aric's wound. *Are you okay to continue, or do you want to go back to the camp?*

Aric looked into his eyes and gestured with his head that he wanted to keep going. *I'll fight to the death. I'm fine.*

Seth nodded, and they trekked on toward the vampire lair.

Armando had sent Jonah and Diana ahead to scope the area out for the rest of them. He figured if he lost them, it wouldn't be that big of a deal. His other soldiers were stronger than the couple.

"My king, do you want us to spread throughout the woods now?" Zephryne inquired.

Armando looked around at his army of thirty vampires who were awaiting his orders. They were hungry for blood, and they were hungry for battle.

"Zephryne, you and I are going to return to the lair to wait for Melanie and the Lycan queen. The rest of you will spread out and fight to the death," he commanded.

The vampires pressed on while thinning out to cover more ground.

"I assume Jonah and Diana were discovered," he mentioned on the walk back to Brad's house.

"Is that why you want to wait there?" she dared to ask.

He shot her a seething stare. "I'm not retreating; I don't cower in the corner when I'm faced with death. I want to wait for the Lycan queen to be delivered to me," he reiterated.

Zephryne doubted that he was telling her the entire truth, but she wouldn't dare say so. "Of course, my king. Please forgive me."

When they reached the house, he had her barricade the door and windows while he flipped through Brad's collection of books and occult items. If there was anything he could do to ensure survival, he would find it there.

Yoska turned toward Ofelia. "What now? Do we find the other Lycans?"

Tressa was sure that's what Ofelia would want, so she replied, "No. I want you to spread out wide. We need to cover any parts of the forest that they aren't."

"With all due respect, we are stronger if we stay together," Jeric, one of the Gypsy warriors, mentioned.

She glared at him. "And I appreciate your concern, but I think I know what I'm doing. Now, spread out and cover the forest."

Unlike with Melanie, Tressa couldn't read Ofelia's thoughts. The Gypsy was doing well to keep them closed off. She could, however, feel the woman's panic, and she fed off it.

"Don't worry, Ofelia, we're going after the vampire king," she spoke aloud. "You'll still get to see some action." She turned in the direction of Brad's house, using the sun as a compass.

Julia and Elmira got lost in the woods when they tried to track down Ofelia and the others.

"She's fast," Julia commented as she tried to figure their location out. "I think we need to find the highway and follow it. That might be our best chance."

"But we have no idea what direction she was headed in," Elmira pointed out.

Julia bit her bottom lip and looked around the vast woods. "That's because we don't know what her agenda is. Is she possessed by someone wanting to kill the Lycans? If so, then we need to find them. If she wants to kill the vampires, then we need to locate them, and in doing so, we should cross paths with Seth and the other Lycans. Therefore, we need to head toward Brad's house because I'm sure that's where Seth was headed."

"Brad?" Elmira inquired.

Julia looked down into her kind but worried face. "He's the dark Gypsy. We have to watch out for him too. He might even be working with the spirit that possessed Ofelia."

Elmira wrung her hands, and her eyes darted nervously. "Oh. I think we should go back to the camp and let the Lycans handle this. I don't want you to risk yourself, my queen."

Julia shook her head in refusal. "A leader who won't fight with their soldiers is no leader at all. If he's taught me anything, Seth has taught me that."

Elmira sighed and patted the queen's hand. "You are very brave. You both are very brave."

"We all have to be," Julia noted and continued on, looking for the highway that would lead to Brad's house.

A loud battle cry rang out from behind them, and Melanie tackled her to the ground. The torch Julia had been holding flew into a small creek and was extinguished.

Julia struggled underneath the vampire's weight and fierce grasp, but she couldn't shake her. She squeezed her eyes closed, anticipating the bite to her neck, when Melanie suddenly yelped and rolled away from her.

Elmira had burned her with her torch, but the vampire rolled on the ground to put out the flames searing her back. Julia scrambled to her feet and took the torch from Elmira to finish the execution, but she hesitated when she looked into her former best friend's eyes.

Melanie noticed the moment of weakness and sprang at her, knocking her down once more.

"You should've just done it," she hissed into Julia's ear while saliva dripped onto her cheek. "I have no problem with killing *you*."

Elmira felt helpless because her torch had gone out also when it hit the grass, which was wet from a rain shower in the early morning hours. She picked it up, however, and began to whack the vampire with it. If she was going to die, she would go down fighting.

Melanie swung her arm at the Gypsy, striking her hard enough to send her flying backward into a large oak tree. Then she descended on Julia, who was still writhing beneath her, and sank her teeth into the woman's neck. She hadn't drunk that much, however, when fierce growling interrupted her. She looked up and met the accusing glare of a pack of wolves. The ferocious animals quickly lunged at her, tackling her backward off Julia, and ripped into her with their gnashing teeth until her violent screams were permanently squelched.

Julia cried out, fearing she was next, but the pack looked at her with a calm demeanor they didn't have before. They looked at her almost the same way Oscar did, and then they ran off.

Clenching her bleeding neck, Julia scrambled to her feet and went to Elmira's side. The woman's head was bleeding, but she was alive. Julia tried pulling Elmira to her feet, but she became lightheaded and slumped to the ground next to her. She realized it was possible she was bleeding to death from Melanie's bite, and desperation overcame her. She did the only thing she felt she could do to survive. She lapped at Elmira's head wound.

She immediately began to feel better, so she got back on her feet and pulled Elmira up with renewed strength. Then she used the lighter in her pocket to relight the torch and touched it down to Melanie's remains. She had to be certain the vampire was dead.

She looked at her hand in wonderment and fear. Her nails had already grown out to incredible lengths. She ran her tongue over her teeth and felt the fangs. She also felt the craving for blood that came with the transformation, and Elmira's head was still bleeding. She squeezed her eyes shut and swallowed back the hunger with a dry gulp. It burned her throat, but she would cope with it.

Elmira came to and stood next to her, trembling, while they looked at Melanie's burning remains. Rain suddenly began to fall, and it extinguished the flames, but they had already done their job. The abrupt shower put out Julia's torch as well.

She looked at it and mumbled, "Well, that takes care of that. I was wondering how to avoid a forest fire."

Elmira studied her as if she recognized that something had changed, but she only asked, "Is that the vampire who bit you before?"

"Yes," Julia whispered, and her hand flew to her neck, but it came back dry. The bleeding had stopped; however, she could still feel the puncture wounds.

"Are you feeling okay now? I see she bit you again," Elmira observed.

Julia kept her lips closed as much as possible, so Elmira wouldn't see her fangs. "I'm fine. Let's keep going."

They crossed the creek and kept heading west toward Brad's house. Julia fought with her hunger the entire time, but she at least felt that she had an edge on the enemy with her newfound strength. That was if the Lycans didn't perceive her as a threat and kill her first.

Seth heard Melanie's death scream, although he didn't know it was her, and he assumed one of the Lycans had taken out one more vampire. He wondered how many were left, but he couldn't begin to guess.

He paused to sniff the air, and the sickly stench of bloodsucker wafted to him on the rain breeze. *There's at least one vampire nearby,* he communicated to the others. *Be prepared.*

A loud rustling in the wet leaves caught his attention as a vampire fell from the trees on top of Gunner. He rushed to the Lycan's side along with two others, but they were too late. The bloodsucker had already ripped his throat out and took off his head with a double-edged dagger.

Seth and the others lunged at the vampire and quickly tore into it before detaching its skull. They shared a moment of silence for their fallen brother and then proceeded through the woods with newfound rage.

Seth considered telling the others about their loss, but he wanted them to stay focused, so he kept it to himself for the time being. His private thoughts were suddenly interrupted by loud cries of pain as another Lycan was attacked. He couldn't tell from where, though, to be of any help. He'd told the group to stay at least two together at all times, so hopefully they had listened.

Minutes later, he heard Caleb. *We're okay, but Kali was jumped by two vampires. We succeeded in destroying them; however, she's injured. It's not serious, though, so we're moving onward.*

Seth breathed a sigh of relief at the news. He couldn't stand the idea of another one of his armies being slaughtered. He'd already failed once, and he'd rather die than see it happen again.

Keep heading west but stay fanned out. We'll surround the Gypsy's house.

Tressa heard footsteps behind her, so she spun around, prepared to fight. It was three of the Gypsy warriors, though, so she let her guard down.

"Why are you following me?" she demanded haughtily. "I told you to spread out."

Milo answered, "We are just worried about you, Ofelia. There's safety in numbers, and you shouldn't be out here alone. There's no need to fight alone."

She looked away from them and rolled her eyes with a deep sigh. There really wasn't any reason they couldn't travel with her. She was just going after Armando and the book of black magic. She wanted the book for a revival spell, so she could completely take over Ofelia's body and live again.

"Fine, you can hunt with me," she relented. "Just don't slow me down."

"We won't," Jeric promised, and the three men walked behind her, matching her stride for stride.

They traveled several yards before a group of three vampires rushed them. The creatures advanced on them with bloodthirsty snarls, and the Gypsies crouched to defend themselves. Tressa relied on Ofelia's lithe body since she didn't have any experience in combat. Her fighting had always been done with spells and curses. That was another reason to get to the book of black magic. She needed a spell to help her seek her revenge on the vampire king.

The vampire lunged at her with its fangs bared, and she quickly ducked to thwart him. She lashed out with the dagger strapped to her side when she recovered her balance, and it sliced open the vampire's thigh. Then she slashed again across the creature's stomach, causing him to stumble backward.

Tressa noticed a flicker of light to her left, and then she watched with pleasure as Jeric finished the creature off for her. He'd relit his torch and set the vampire on fire. The other two vampires were burned as well.

She looked at him and smiled for the first time. "Thank you. I guess I needed your help after all."

He narrowed his eyes at her but returned her smile. "You're welcome. Shall we continue?"

Tressa nodded and continued leading the way to Brad's dwelling. They'd be there soon.

Julia and Elmira stumbled over vines and logs while trying to get to the highway. "I don't think we're ever going to find the damn road," Julia spat. "I think we're just walking in circles."

"Everything does look the same," Elmira agreed. "Don't give up, though."

Julia groaned, "I won't," just as they heard a commotion not too far away from them.

Both women tensed up, expecting vampires to come leaping at them. The air was eerily calm since the rain had passed, and Julia sniffed it to see if she could smell Lycans or vampires. She smelled old blood and imagined that it was the distinguishing scent of vampires. There was no sense in putting it off.

She pointed north. "We need to go that way I think," she stated and once again swallowed back the burning in her throat. She craved fresh blood, and she didn't know how long she could continue to fight it. Ignoring the natural desires of the monster she'd become was taking all her strength. "I think the sound came from that way," she added, so Elmira wouldn't be suspicious.

Elmira shrugged and followed her, still clutching the potion bottle she would use on Ofelia when they found her.

Julia's senses were as sharp as her new teeth. She could see farther, and her hearing picked up every sound. She heard the flutter of bird wings and the beating of a stag's heart. She spotted the huge buck in the distance before he saw her and scurried off. Its blood didn't call to her, however, so she let it be.

"Oh, that deer scared me," Elmira exclaimed and put her hand over her heart. "I thought it was a vampire."

Julia couldn't help but think the worse scenario for her would've been a Lycan. *What about my husband? Will he have to destroy me?*

She heard a rattling noise nearby and snapped out of her reverie. Elmira was about to step on a rattlesnake, which was prepared to strike, so without thinking, Julia lunged at it. She grasped it and flung it far away from them before it could bite her twice.

"Oh, my lord!" Elmira stared at the bite on Julia's hand with bulging eyes. "We have to do something."

Julia held her hand up and turned it over. "It's all right, Elmira. I'm fine." She glanced at the woman's ashen face and went on to explain, "I was going to die earlier after Melanie bit me again. I became dizzy, and my heart was slowing down."

Elmira's jaw fell open, making her look like a fish out of water. Her hand flew to her head wound, which was sticky from the blood, and she put everything together.

"You drank my blood," she uttered in disbelief.

Julia opened her arms in a shrug. "I had to because I was going to die. I'm not going to hurt you, though. I would never do that. I'd rather set myself on fire with this torch." She held the object up to make her point.

Elmira's eyes fixated on the dancing flames. "I believe you," she replied. "But what about—"

"The Lycans?" Julia finished. "I'm worried about that too. For now, though, I just have to use my new strength to fight. Before it gets dark, we need to keep going."

They traveled in silence for several yards when Julia smelled copper. She knew it was a vampire because it was the metallic stench of death. She held her hand up to halt Elmira.

"There's a vampire close by," she whispered and took slow steps forward.

Elmira clutched the torch hard enough to turn her knuckles white, waving it back and forth in front of her like a death threat.

A snapping of twigs made Julia turn to the right just as two vampires sprang at them. She locked grips with one while the other circled Elmira like a shark in bloody waters. The vampire hissed, showing its fangs, so she returned the gesture, catching the other creature off guard. She found the inner strength to spring in that second and wrapped her hands around the vampire's neck. With a squeeze and hard twist, she broke it and then kept going until the head ripped off. The whole encounter took under a minute.

She spun around and lunged at the other one, which was still engaged in a dance of death with Elmira. The force of her tackle knocked the creature into the torch, setting it ablaze, and its screams pierced the thick vegetation, drawing out another three vampires.

They eyed Julia through narrow slits and immediately perceived her as the biggest threat. What they couldn't figure out, though, was why she was a threat when she was clearly one of them.

"Who are you?" the larger male hissed. "Why are you with a human?"

Julia was ready to pounce. "I'm your enemy," she returned and leapt before the vampire could process her words. As soon as they hit the ground, she buried her fangs into its neck, tearing its jugular out.

A blow to her back made her collapse on the twitching body, and she quickly rolled away before being struck again. She sprang to her feet, evading a second blow, and bounced off a tree like a torpedo with her claws out. She crashed into her target with an audible thud, knocking the creature back on its ass. Before the female had time to recover, Julia kicked her in the head with enough force to crack her skull. Then she wrestled with her, putting her in a death grip, and mutilated her throat too.

The third vampire had his mouth close to Elmira's neck, but Julia intercepted in time by kicking him off her friend. The male vampire tried to come back at them, but Julia leapt at the same time he did, and their bodies clashed together like thunder. She fell backward to the ground, so he used the chance to spring at Elmira again.

The Gypsy tried to run away, but the vampire was too quick, and Julia still had the wind knocked out of her. The vampire was close to piercing the woman's skin when a Lycan broke through the trees and yanked it off. Its clawed hand swiped across the vampire's throat and then again across its face. Elmira finished it and the other two off by setting them on fire.

The Lycan turned toward Julia and cocked its head in confusion. She held her breath, waiting for its fatal pounce, but the huge beast didn't make a move.

"Stop! It's not what you think," Elmira yelped. "She won't hurt any of us."

The Lycan slowly paced the ground in front of Julia, and then it turned to walk off in the direction it had come.

"Wait," she called out after it, and it spun back around. She held her arm out. "Bite me, so I don't have to be this-this thing. I don't want to be a vampire."

Again, the creature cocked its head at her, and it made no move to follow her request.

"As your queen, I demand you do this for me," she asserted. "Just one bite, so I can become Lycan."

The huge beast slowly approached her and complied with her demand. She screamed and yanked her bloody arm back in pain. Then she gawked at it as the torturous transformation from woman to beast began. She felt like her skin was being ripped away with hot knives. Her bones popped loudly as they stretched and molded to build a new frame. Her gums felt like they were on fire as sharper, longer teeth sprouted. She felt like she was slowly dying as her body mangled itself into something new.

When the agony was over, her heavy panting slowed down, along with her pounding heart, and she looked at her surroundings with fresh eyes for the second time that day. Her sense of smell was sharper than the vampire's, and her eyes could see for miles. She looked at the other Lycan and at Elmira and nodded with her head for them to keep going.

Seth had heard the agonizing screams, but he assumed it was a vampire being slaughtered, which was what he was doing right then too. He and Yanko were fighting off a pack of four bloodsuckers, and it wasn't easy. First, they knocked away the weapons the vampires carried, and then he picked two vampires up at once and crashed them into each other while Yanko was dodging the other two. Snarls, gasps, and growls filled the muggy air as they took turns assaulting each other.

Seth crouched to dodge one attacker while the other he'd been battling slid underneath him and bit into his muscled thigh. He howled from the pain and dug his claws into the vampire's torso to rip out its heart. Then he spun around in circles to get the other one off his back. That didn't work, and he felt the sting of fangs again, so he quickly bent over, flinging the vampire over his head. He grabbed both of its arms and pulled until they detached. The head followed.

Yanko, unfortunately, wasn't faring as well. He'd been badly torn into, and it didn't look like he'd hold on much longer. Seth clutched his arms around the remaining vampire and squeezed until he heard the snap of its spine. Then he yanked the head until it detached.

He knelt next to Yanko's slumped body. *I'm sorry I couldn't get to you sooner, my friend.*

Yanko looked at him with sad eyes. *I'm sorry I failed you, King Seth. I don't think I can go on. Please just leave me here and go save the others.*

Seth shook his head and picked his soldier up to carry him on his back. As long as Yanko's heart beat, there was a chance to save him. They could use Gypsy magic when they returned to camp.

Tressa was tired of walking, so she stopped and told the men she needed a rest. She slumped against a tree that looked the same as all the other trees. She hoped they were headed in the right direction because everything looked the same.

"I'm going to scout some terrain to the east," Jeric announced and took off in a trot before anyone could object.

He traveled a quarter mile before stumbling onto Elmira roaming with two Lycans. "Elmira, I'm glad to see you," he panted. "I've been walking with Ofelia and two others, and something is wrong with our leader. She isn't acting like her usual self."

Elmira held her hand up to stop him. "I'm aware of the situation, but I'm glad you saw it too. I'm sure she's been possessed, and I have a potion to save her." She held up the small bottle for emphasis. "Take us to her."

On the brisk walk back, he asked, "Why are you out here? I thought you stayed back at the camp for your safety."

She nodded and explained, "I'm out here with our queen. The smaller Lycan with us is none other than Queen Julia. We came to help Ofelia with an exorcism."

Jeric's eyes bulged as he looked at the Lycan. "Does the king know about her?"

"No, we've not found him or the others yet. The large Lycan with us crossed our path and followed her command to turn her," Elmira answered. "There's more to the story, but that's all you need to know for now."

When they reached the area Ofelia had stopped at, she and the others were gone. Jeric knew it was the right spot because of a huge fallen maple tree.

"They were right here," he said and gestured to the grass. "But we were heading northwest, and I'm sure they haven't gotten far."

Julia sniffed the air for humans, but there was a confusing mingle of odors. She followed Jeric and Elmira, keeping herself fully alert to danger. They traveled a hundred yards when they finally caught up to Ofelia, Milo, and Carlisle.

"What are you doing out here?" Tressa demanded of Elmira while keeping a wary eye on the Lycans.

"I've come to help," Elmira answered. "It's my people out here too."

Tressa rolled her eyes at the woman. "Whatever but you aren't going to slow us down." She turned her back on the Gypsy, who took the opportunity to throw the potion at her while chanting an exorcism prayer in Latin. "What are you doing to me?" Tressa shrieked as she felt herself being evicted from Ofelia's body.

"I'm saving my friend and leader," Elmira answered with a smile as the black aura rose from Ofelia's body and then burst into a thousand particles. She looked at the men and Ofelia and announced, "The evil spirit is gone. It won't be possessing anyone else."

"Thank you," Ofelia gasped while looking at her hands with relief. She could finely feel and use her body again. "It was awful. I felt like I was being suffocated by her."

"Her? Do you know who she was?" Elmira wondered.

"Yes, it was Tressa, the evil witch who'd abducted me from the dark Gypsy," she replied and looked at all their faces, including the Lycans'.

Elmira followed her gaze and pointed to the smaller Lycan. "This is Julia."

Ofelia's brows shot up. "Oh? I didn't realize she'd wanted to become Lycan." She looked at Jeric and asked, "How far are we from camp?"

He shrugged. "Several miles I think, but I'm not familiar with this terrain. Do you want to go back?"

Her mouth turned down. "The witch wanted revenge on Armando. She told me that much."

"But you should leave that fight to the Lycans," Elmira asserted. "I think the warriors are needed at the camp. I think trying to fight alongside the Lycans will only distract them."

Ofelia bit her bottom lip and considered their options. "That may be true, however, the warriors are all spread out per the witch's demand. I couldn't possibly get them all back to camp. I think we should just keep going and see this through. It's our battle too"—she met Elmira's concerned stare—"Of course, you can always go back if you like. The men will take you."

Elmira shook her head emphatically. "No, you're right. This is our fight too, and that includes me. I should be of some help."

Ofelia gave her older friend a beaming smile. "You've already helped so much. Thank you again." She gestured to the woods and addressed Julia. "Do you know how to get to the dark Gypsy's lair? Personally, I don't remember where it is."

Julia bobbed her shaggy head and pointed north. Then she led the way with the others following closely behind. She sniffed the air, and the mingling scents of copper and smoke told her they weren't far from their destination.

Seth found Lobo, Brody, Rahl, and Aric a mile farther into the forest. Yanko hadn't survived his wounds, so Seth had dug a crude grave and buried him several yards back.

He explained to the others. *He fought well, and I'd hoped to get him to the Gypsies in time.*

Lobo spoke for his group. *We'll honor him in prayer when this is over. Sadly, he doubtfully will be the only one.*

Seth nodded, already knowing that was the case. He went ahead and told them about Gunner, so they'd know how many Lycans they were already down. They bowed their heads for their fallen comrades and then proceeded on their journey. Seth knew they were close to Brad's house, and the smell of vampires burned their nostrils.

Brody pointed to the left, while Seth pointed to the right. The vampires were circling around them, which was a tactical maneuver Seth had wanted to use on them. Boxing in the enemy was a powerful move. The five Lycans moved in a tight formation, ready for an attack from every side.

Seth mentally called out to the others. *If you're close by, we need your help. A large group of vampires is about to attack, and we're almost to the lair.*

He knew his soldiers would find them by sniffing the battle scene out. He just hoped it would be in time. Suddenly, the air grew calm and quiet—too quiet. Not even the leaves moved. Then things changed, and all hell broke loose.

A group of nine vampires charged at them from all sides, and most of them had bladed weapons. The Lycans ducked, jumped, and rolled out of the way to avoid being sliced in two. Then they pounced at the vampires to turn the tides.

Seth was in a battle with two of the bloodsuckers, when one dropped the samurai sword it was wielding. Seth dove for it and made a red ruin of the vampire's chest before slicing off the head. The second vampire tried to run away, but Seth threw the weapon with deadly precision, burying it in the creature's skull.

The fighting went on for what seemed like forever with screams and blood thickening the air. Thankfully, a few more Lycans had shown up to even the battle out, and in the end, they were the victors. They'd sustained their own injuries, but nothing was life-threatening. Once they caught their breath, they marched the final half-mile to the lair, only hesitating to kill a few more vampires along the way.

They were joined by the other Lycans, who'd heard Seth's call to arms while following the retreating vampires.

Julia, Ofelia, Elmira, the other Lycan, and the three Gypsy men came within view of Brad's house. They'd heard the nearby screams and knew the ultimate battle would soon be going down. The sun hung low in the sky, casting it in shades of pink and orange, but they could only see blood-red. They snuck around the back of the house to lie in wait for the enemy or their allies, whichever arrived first.

Julia smelled the heavy scent of dead blood and knew the house was swarming with vampires, including the king. In her Lycan state, though, she couldn't tell the others in her group.

She feared changing back because of the pain she'd have to endure again and also because she had no clothes to put on. However, she couldn't let her people down, so she ducked behind a tree and shifted back. While still extremely painful, it wasn't as bad as the first change. Nonetheless, she bit her tongue to avoid screaming out and alerting the enemy.

"Ofelia," she whispered, and the Gypsy leader rushed to her. "I wanted to warn you that I can smell the vampires inside the house, including the king. At least I think I smelled him. Anyway, I just wanted to make you aware."

Ofelia nodded. "I assumed as much but thank you. I know your transformation had to be very painful."

Julia was about to answer, but a loud hiss behind her made her spin around to face the enemy. Thankfully, it was only one vampire, but he was a large one, and she had no weapons and no time to shift back.

The drooling creature took in the lovely sight of her body and licked his lips. "Well, don't you look tasty?" he sneered. "I might have to satisfy two thirsts."

Before he could lunge at her, Ofelia dove at him and buried her dagger into his throat, turning it into a fountain of flashing red. She didn't stop there, though. She twisted the blade until it drilled through the backside. Then she vigorously performed a sawing motion until the head detached. Luckily, his bloody cries were nothing more than gurgles, so no other vampires showed up.

Julia took a deep breath and focused on the beast inside her, so the change would come. It hurt as first, but the pain didn't last as long as before, and it was becoming bearable. She rejoined the others when the transformation was complete.

"We haven't seen anyone coming or going," Carlisle whispered to her while passing his dagger from hand to hand. He was clearly ready to battle.

Julia heard howling nearby, and her heart fluttered. It had to be Seth and the others. It was time to prove herself worthy of her crown.

Armando nervously paced the living room in Brad's house. He assumed some of his soldiers were dead, but he couldn't guess how many. He also had no knowledge of how many Lycans had been killed off because no one in his army had reported back to him. He could sense it in the air that the finale was coming. Luckily, he'd found a spell to help him prepare. He'd found a spell that would undoubtedly save his immortal life.

Loud yelps outside let him know that his army had retreated to the lair, so he looked at Zephryne to tell her to unbarricade the door. He halted, however, when louder screams mixed with growls announced the enemy's presence. He shook his head at her and walked to the darkened window to witness the carnage.

The vampires formed a protective line in front of the house, and likely on the sides and rear too, but the Lycans advanced upon them.

Seth looked at the others and conveyed his thoughts. *To the end.*

They all replied in kind, and somehow, it gave him the inner strength he needed to finish. He threw his head back and let out a deafening howl, and his army charged the vampires. The horror began.

Julia and the Gypsies aggressively fought the vampires that had appeared out of nowhere. The howl she'd heard strengthened the Lycan queen for the battle, and she gave it everything she had. Blow after blow, she beat her enemies down. Blood flowed in crimson petals from large, gaping wounds, and the stench of copper filled the muggy air, burning the insides of their nostrils, and they didn't let up.

As the bloodsuckers fell, Elmira set them on fire with her protective torch until a ghastly inferno raged all around them. Sadly, Milo received a fatal blow by sword and fell into the flames too. They couldn't stop battling to mourn him, though. It would have to wait until they could mourn all their losses.

Once they sent the last vampire in the group to hell, they carefully maneuvered around to the front of the house to fight alongside their other comrades.

Julia breathed a deep sigh of relief when she saw Seth. He was heavily engaged in hand to hand combat, but at least he was alive. She was about to rush to his side, but a vampire lunged and tackled her to the ground. She sustained a deep bite to the shoulder before her red claws raked the vampire's cheek, scratching for its eyes. The vampire screeched in pain but didn't pause its assault. It sank its teeth into her neck and tried to tear her throat, but she gained leverage and thrust it off her into a large elm tree. Before it could recover, she thrashed her claws across its body with both hands, shredding flesh and bone, until she got to the heart. She yanked it out and tossed it into the woods. The head soon followed, rolling away from the spurting stump.

She was attacked by two more vampires as the last shred of light left the sky. They both had a firm grip on her, sinking in their fangs, so she thrashed her body to get them off. Refusing to let go, they continued tearing into her. Desperate, she ran into a tree to knock them off, but one still clung to her with a death grip. Another Lycan jumped from behind it and swiped across the back of its head, tearing open bone and brain. Crowned in crimson, Julia escaped while the other Lycan finished the task.

She looked for her mate and found him struggling underneath a pile of three vampires. She quickly pounced and violently thrashed her claws to get the bloodsuckers off. Seth seized the moment to tear into the abdomen of one while chomping into the neck of the other, and she helped him by destroying the third.

Seth stood to his full height, panting while the taste of copper filled his mouth. He didn't know who the other Lycan was, but he was grateful and gave his comrade a single nod before they both returned to battle.

Several exhausting minutes later, the circumference of the house was littered with remains. Most of the corpses were vampires, but a few Lycans had fallen in the name of their king. Seth wasn't finished, though. He still had the vampire king to destroy.

He commanded his tired soldiers to keep going. *The king must be inside the house, so we need to storm it together in case he has more soldiers in there as well. I, however, will deal with him, so don't attack.*

They bowed their heads in subservience and rushed the front door and windows. The loud splintering of wood and glittering shards of glass rang through the night as the barriers were destroyed. The Lycans filled the house, sniffing out the enemy, and Seth followed. The stench told him that while vampires had certainly occupied the dwelling, there weren't but a few left if even that many. Curiously, he didn't see any sign of Melanie.

With a loud battle cry, a female vampire suddenly rushed him from another room, and she was swinging a battle axe over her head, preparing to deliver a deadly blow. When the axe came down, he jumped backward and then dove, picking up a large chunk of glass which he swung back around, drawing a savage red line across her pale throat. Another Lycan jumped on her back and twisted her wobbly head off before she had time to recover from her gaping wound.

The Lycan looked at Seth and mentally told him the house was clear of other bloodsuckers.

Except for the king. He has to be here somewhere, and he's mine.

He started to walk into the master bedroom when a slow applause rang out behind him. He spun around to face the vampire king.

Armando eyed the pendant of λύκος. "So, we meet at last, King of the Lycans," he sneered, and Seth answered with a threatening growl. "I guess this is where it ends...for you."

Seth jumped forward at the vampire, but something made him fall short, and he landed on the floor with a loud thud.

The vampire king laughed heartily, and then he was the one who lunged. He tackled Seth and bit into his arm, which was held up in self-defense.

Seth yelped and tried to throw the vampire off himself, but it felt like invisible restraints were holding him down. It felt like his arms were pinned to his sides. Something was very wrong.

The vampire rolled off and stood up of his free will. Then he kicked Seth hard in the gut, causing more yelps.

"You can't hurt me," the king hissed. "So, don't bother summoning your lackeys because they can't hurt me either, and they will just die with you." He reared his foot back and delivered a crushing kick to the side of Seth's head. "You see, I cast a spell to protect myself from your kind. There's nothing you can do, so I think I'll take my sweet time in destroying you and your army. Does that make two times you failed now or three?" he jeered.

Seth let out a low, throaty growl in response. Then he noticed something over Armando's shoulder. Two of his soldiers had come back to help him.

He screamed at them to stop. *Don't! Black magic is at play, and he'll kill you. He cast a spell to stop us from attacking him. Get everyone and retreat!*

One of the Lycans ignored his plea, though, and swiped his claws at the back of the vampire's neck. Or at least he tried to. His gesture fell short, and the vampire spun around to return the attack, ripping the Lycan's throat out.

"I'm immune to Lycans," he spat in the dying soldier's face while the other one ran off. After finishing the deed, he turned back to Seth and sneered, "I can't wait to find your queen when I'm done with you. Killing her is going to be such a pleasure. I'm really looking forward to it, almost as much as I'm looking forward to this." He leaned over Seth, prepared to bury his fangs in the Lycan king's throat, but footsteps halted him and made him look back at the doorway. Seth looked too, and his heart almost stopped.

Julia, standing proud and naked, stood in the doorway with a smirk. "I hear you're looking for me," she ground out between clenched teeth.

Armando rose to his feet and bowed to her. "You must be the elusive Lycan queen. I must say, you positively radiate beauty, but if you think you can seduce me into sparing your husband, you're dead wrong."

Julia laughed softly, confidently. "You say that you can survive a Lycan's attack, but you never counted on me," she hissed at him. "I'm a breed you're not going to survive."

Both he and Seth gawked when she smiled to show off her vampire fangs, but then Armando regained his composure. "Even if you're a vampire now, that doesn't mean you can hurt me, darling. I've got years' worth of experience on you," he pointed out in a sadistic tone.

She held her smile in place. "I'm not a vampire, though, Armando. I'm a half-breed. I'm part vampire and part Lycan," she seethed and leapt at him, biting the fingers off the hand he held up in self-defense.

She had him pinned to the floor next to Seth, who was bleeding profusely, and she didn't let up in the attack. She knew she had to quickly dispatch him, so she could save her husband's life. She quickly dipped her head and tore into his jugular, tugging as hard as she could to rip it out. She found herself missing the Lycan's strength as she thrashed her head back and forth. Blood sprayed in her face, and he clawed at her back and arms to throw her off, but she held fast. Then he brought a knee up to her chest and thrust her backward against the wall. She quickly recovered, however, and flung herself at him again as he tried to stand up. She dug her claws into his sides and ripped them across the front to meet in the middle, spilling out his guts. When he collapsed, she dropped to the floor, grabbed his head, and twisted until his neck cracked. She was about to chomp into his throat again, wanting to destroy the tendons keeping his head intact, when Seth bolted upright. He was in human form, and he reached out and took over. With one brisk powerful twist, the vampire king's head was removed. He tossed the foul appendage across the room with a look of satisfaction. Then he turned to his wife, and his eyes were spilling over with questions.

"How did this happen? Please explain how this came to be," he finally verbalized his thoughts.

Julia swallowed back her worries and slowly explained, "Ofelia was attacked and possessed by an evil spirit, so Elmira and I followed her and the men into the woods to undo the dark magic with a potion. Melanie attacked me, though, and drained me to the point of death. The only way to survive was to drink some of Elmira's blood, so I did. However, I couldn't remain this way, being this *thing*, so I had a Lycan bite me. I know it must deeply trouble you, but I promise I've not attacked anyone, and I no longer have that particular thirst." She looked at him with love-softened eyes that begged for his understanding.

His mouth turned up into a soft smile, and he squeezed her hand. "I love you no matter what you are, and you saved my life, so I suppose it's a good thing you're a hybrid."

Her brow quirked, and she grinned. "Hybrid? I like that word better than half-breed."

He rose to his feet and helped her up, eyeing her body up and down. "Now who's running around naked?" he teased.

She laughed and pointed at his nude body. "I guess we both are."

He laughed too and glanced at Brad's closet. "I suppose we could borrow his clothes," he suggested. "He won't be needing them anymore." He grabbed a shirt from the closet and tore it into shreds to make a tourniquet for his bleeding arm.

Julia looked curiously at him. "Is he dead then?"

Seth smiled smugly. "Yes, Mei came across him while he was disguised to look like Ofelia. He was coming after you. She saw through it, though, and attacked him, and then I finished him off."

She breathed a sigh of relief. "Well, good. I won't ever have to worry about him again."

He tilted her chin up and leaned down to kiss her. "You won't have to worry about anyone or anything again, my luscious queen," he breathed against her lips.

"My hero," she sighed while happiness filled her heart.

After he tore himself away from her mouth, he gestured toward the doorway. "The others are waiting on us, so we should get dressed."

Julia wrinkled her nose, and she glanced at the closet. "I don't want to smell like Brad."

Seth's eyes crinkled when he laughed. "We could always shift and run back that way," he suggested.

She looked up at the ceiling and nodded. "Okay since it's not hurting so bad now."

He reached for her arm to stop her, though. "I can mentally communicate with my pack, but I never read your thoughts," he mumbled.

She cocked her head. "Maybe it's the vampire part of me that blocked you."

He shrugged his broad muscled shoulders, which had already stopped bleeding through the crude bandages. "I suppose. I'll have to try again, so concentrate with me."

They quickly shifted, and she was almost as fast as him. He looked into her eyes and projected his thoughts. *Can you hear me, Julia?*

She bobbed her furry head and used her thoughts to reply that she could. Then she heard the thoughts of the others who were anxiously waiting outside. Hand in hand, they exited the house, and Seth told them that the vampire king was destroyed, and the Lycan by his side was his queen. Raucous howling filled the air as they bayed in unison. It caused the nearby wildlife to scatter, but it brought forth the pack of wolves that had rescued her from Melanie.

Feeling a rooted connection to them, Julia tentatively approached the alpha and placed her hand on its head. *Thank you.* She didn't know if the creature heard her thoughts, but it whined in response.

Seth smiled inside at the lovely vision, and then he looked around at the happy Gypsy faces, including Elmira's, and told his army that it was time to get back to the camp.

When he took his first step, he heard his wife's taunt. *Race you back.*

April 19, 2014

Julia woke up with a light heart and a wide smile. When her eyes fluttered open, she found her husband staring at her.

"Someone woke up in a good mood," he purred and stroked her red tendrils.

"That's because I have a lot to be grateful for," she replied, still smiling. "I can't believe how well everything turned out. I mean, some people died, and I had to fend off my best friend from killing me, but all in all, it turned out much better than I thought it would."

Seth feigned surprise. "I can't believe you doubted me. I told you it would all be okay."

She shrugged. "Well, you can understand my lack of faith when I had fangs dug into my neck, and then I saw them dug into yours."

He brushed her hair aside. "I know, and I'm sorry I wasn't there to protect you from Melanie. I'm just happy the pack of wolves came to your rescue," he murmured.

She glanced at her dog and added, "Don't forget Oscar. He saved me from her first."

"Oh, I would never forget my boy," Seth chuckled and ruffled the dog's fur. "I'm going to let him outside, so I can have some alone time with Mommy," he cooed and climbed out of bed to open the door for Oscar.

"Alone time, huh?" she teased. "What would you like to do with me that he can't witness?"

Seth grinned. "I'm going to show you the animal I really am."

He pinned her arms over her head and proved he was the alpha of their pack, washing her body in love and erotic love play.

He drove into her welcoming body with an urgent need to possess every bit of her. She was warm, soft, damp, and all his.

Julia closed her eyes as tension coiled inside her and then released in a white-hot wave. Liquid fire singed her veins in a scorching blaze as the multiple orgasms tore through her. She was gripped with mindless ecstasy mingled with a deep, burning love, and she couldn't stop the single tear from rolling down her cheek. She reached out to caress his face and then ran her hands over his massive shoulders, biceps, and torso as his muscles rippled underneath her touch. Then something inside her took over, and she thrashed against him. It was the beast, and it wanted to play. She wrapped her leg around his and pushed on his chest, flipping him over onto his back.

He grinned seductively at her as she straddled his hips. Then her silken sheath clenched around his hot steel as she slid herself down it. Her muscles spasmed, and her entire body shuddered while her head tilted back in soundless ecstasy. She rocked her hips violently back and forth, riding each crashing wave of pleasure until the abyss completely swallowed her.

Seth clenched his hands on her hips, guiding her up and down his shaft as he spiraled toward his own release. The rush soon built within him, and he struggled to hold on just a little longer. The need to explode built inside him until he could restrain it no longer, and he pounded home, bursting within her and filling her with his love.

They embraced each other while heavily panting from their pleasure. He ran his fingertips over her arm and side while hers played on his chest. When sleep tugged at him, he lazily sat upright.

"Before I fall back to sleep, we should probably make an appearance. I think we might be saying good-bye to some of the pack today," he told her.

Julia felt sad. "I hope not. I'm rather fond of everyone."

He climbed out of bed with a groan. "I am too, but now that the battle is over, they might want to go back to their homelands. I can't force them to stay."

She got out of the warm bed too and sighed. "I suppose not. Still...I'll miss them."

They quickly dressed and met the others in time for breakfast. Oscar was already being hand-fed by some of the children, and Julia watched the amusing spectacle with fresh eyes.

She turned to Seth and told him, "I think I'm ready."

He quirked a brow and followed her gaze. "For what exactly?" he asked with hope in his heart.

She rubbed his arm and sighed, "For a child."

He beamed at her, and the amber flecks danced in his eyes. "That's wonderful to hear. I am too."

She placed her hand on her stomach. "I'll stop taking the pill then." She looked up with concern. "Do you think they'll be hybrids like me?"

He laughed and wrapped his arm tightly around her trim waist. "I sure hope so because I want them to resemble their beautiful mother."

She blushed and looked down. "I just hope they're the best parts of both of us."

He smiled at her and then cleared his throat to get everyone's attention. "I want to say, first of all, thank you for your loyal support during these trying days. Be proud of yourselves because I'm proud of you. You all helped fulfill the prophecy and saved the world. Secondly, I want us to remember our fallen brothers and sisters with love. Godspeed Gunner, Yanko, Halley, Mason, Milo, and Netta. May your souls live on forever."

Everyone bowed their head as Elmira led them in prayer. Then he continued, "I hope the Lycans will stay here with us, but I understand if you want to go back to your homes."

Lobo rose from his seat and announced on behalf of his group, "If the Gypsy tribe doesn't mind us hanging around, we'd love to stay and support our king."

The other Lycan clans emphatically agreed, and Ofelia told them they were certainly welcomed to stay with them.

Julia had something to say too. "I want us to purchase a house in the woods and the surrounding land. That way, you'll all have a place to camp and hunt."

Seth looked up and replied, "That's a wonderful idea. Shall we go house hunting?"

She smiled down at her handsome husband and winked. "No need. I already made an offer on James's home, and the family accepted. We can move in immediately."

He cocked his head and told her, "So, you did trust me then. You trusted me to see you safely through the battle."

She chuckled and plopped back down next to him. "Yes, I trusted you and saw a future."

Please review on Amazon

Visit Alexis's website:
http://bit.do/AlexisKennedy

- ♥ Leave a comment
- ♥ Watch trailers
- ♥ See what's coming next
- ♥ Check out reviews
- ♥ Check out the blog

Thanks for your continued support!

Turn the page for a peek at Angry House

PROLOGUE

BROOKLYN, NY

Rhett Shaw stared at the blank screen in front of himself while Mötley Crüe blared on the stereo in the background. He ran his calloused hands over his tired eyes and leaned back, forcing the chair to make an awful creaking sound. This had become a habit lately, and his editor wasn't any happier about it than he was. He rose from the chair and crossed the room to look out the window at the crowded city streets of Brooklyn below. He was tired of that sight, of those sounds, and of the smell of Chinese food mixed with curry—he was tired of life here. He no longer had ties to this city.

Laura, his wife, had passed away almost three years ago, which was when he'd quit his full-time job as a carpenter and become the reclusive writer he was now. He'd been working on his first book when she died, and she'd always been such an encouragement to him that he knew he needed to finish it no matter what—he owed it to her—so he quit his day job and burned the midnight oil until it was finished in a matter of months. Wolfsbane was a hit too, and so was its successor, Wolfsbane—The Blood of Dragons. He'd not received any movie deals, yet, but they were still performing much better in sales than he'd expected, and now his editor expected another hit from him and pronto. But here he was with nary a word. Every time he'd write a sentence, or even a whole paragraph, he'd end up changing his mind and erasing the whole thing—nothing was sticking. He supposed this was the norm, and he'd just gotten lucky on his first two books. Of course, it could also be because he was trying his hand at crime fiction this time—he wanted a break from paranormal romance. He didn't think he could write any more romance when his heart was still breaking.

His feeling of frustration brought him around to the idea of making other changes once more, and his gray eyes scanned the tiny fifth floor apartment. In the hall closet, there was still an orderly stack of moving boxes from when he had moved in one month ago. He had kept them because he wanted to try the place out first. The truth was, no place felt like home without Laura, and that just made it even easier to leave. He grabbed the stack of boxes and packed.

ONE

Rhett waved good-bye to his friend Jeremy, who was going to sublease his apartment, which he left fully furnished aside from a small writing desk that was now stuffed inside the back of his 2010 Jeep Grand Cherokee. He left most of the dishes and linens behind as well. Laura had been the cook, and he'd been surviving mostly on beans, weenies, and soup with crackers since her death. If it weren't for the calories from the added assortment of packaged junk food and takeout he bought, he would've wasted away long before now.

Twelve stoplights later, Rhett looked up into the rearview mirror and mentally waved good-bye to Brooklyn. He was on I-95 and would cross the Vermont border in just a few hours. He had no destination in mind—he figured he'd know the place when he saw it. A map lay neatly folded next to him in the passenger seat just in case he got lost, though. Then again, he thought, maybe that's what he needed—to just get lost somewhere where no one knew him. It's not as if he was really leaving anyone behind. He reflected on how Jeremy was really the only person he kept in touch with from his previous life. His face fell as he thought about how disappointed in him Laura would be. She would certainly be heartbroken to see that he'd lost so many friends all because of her death. Rhett's friends had tried to be there for him while he grieved, but his all-consuming sadness had just pushed them away. That's when the writing really took over for him. His therapist, in his one visit, said it was probably because that was his way to escape the pain of reality. Lately, however, he felt used and dried-up—exhausted—while trying to write.

He was still reflecting hours later as he slowly drove past the houses dotting the city streets of Bondville, Vermont, and he dug deep to find a glimmer of hope—a piece of the former life he led when things had felt like some resemblance of "normal." Then he made a silent promise to himself to change his ways. Of course, he'd have to start slowly, so finding a place in town was not ideal for him. For now, he needed to avoid the noise—the crowds—so he just kept on driving. He would find a place in the country to rent or buy and hope that the privacy and quiet would inspire him. Of course, it wouldn't help him reconnect to society, but he could always work on that part later—he needed to get his book done first. His resolution made him feel better.

He kept his eyes peeled for realty signs, and he did find a couple of places to mark on his map. One was even having an open house, so he made the stop.

"Hello there. I'm Tom Kidd, the seller's realtor," said a portly man with silver hair edging his otherwise balding scalp, and he extended a thick meaty hand to Rhett.

Rhett looked down at the hand before taking it. "Hello. I was driving by and saw the house," he replied with a sense of uneasiness.

Mr. Kidd looked at the packed Jeep and gave a small nod in its direction. "It looks like you are all ready to move in," he observed.

Rhett's gaze followed his and then dropped down to his shoes. "Well, I'm trying to find a place."

"I notice an accent. Where are you from? New York, right?"

"Yes, I'm moving from Brooklyn," Rhett confirmed.

"So, you're a city boy, huh? What are you doing out in the sticks then?" Mr. Kidd prodded.

There was no way Rhett was going to tell the man his life story—he was not that kind of person—so, he instead just replied with, "I'm looking for a change." It was true after all.

The realtor chuckled, "I'm sure it'll be quite the change for you. We aren't fast paced around these parts like you New Yorkers are."

Now it was Rhett's turn to chuckle. Nothing about him was fast paced these days; in fact, he'd probably fit right in with the locals. He looked around the yard at the shrubs and flowers as well as the foundation of the two-story brick house. It was bigger than he needed, and a tear stung his eyes as he could hear voices inside his head telling him, "You are young. You could remarry and have a family someday." But he knew he wouldn't. No one would ever replace the empty hole in his heart left by Laura. No one could complete that part of his life again.

"So, like I was saying, the house is ready to move in, and the owners have left wiggle room on the price," Mr. Kidd said, interrupting his thoughts. He'd been talking the entire time, but Rhett had briefly tuned him out.

"Umm," Rhett mumbled and looked up at the house while running a hand over his stubble-covered chin. "I'm sorry, but it's just too damn big." Then, without further explanation, he spun on his heel and jogged to the Jeep with more tears in his eyes. *How the hell can I think about moving on?*

He headed farther north down Hwy B and saw more homes up for sale, but he kept driving nonetheless. Maybe he was thinking too big right now. Maybe an apartment or loft would make the best choice for him. Then, after about another four miles and five turns, he found it—his new home.

www.ingramcontent.com/pod-product-compliance
Lightning Source LLC
Chambersburg PA
CBHW022126170626
46808CB00002B/855